D1577078

Miss Holly
1803
Nigel Kirkwood

HOLLY HOBBIE

RICHARD DUBELMAN

GRANADA
London Toronto Sydney New York

Granada Publishing Limited
Frogmore, St. Albans, Herts AL2 2NF
and
3 Upper James Street, London WIR 4BP
866 United Nations Plaza, New York, NY 10017, USA
117 York Street, Sydney, NSW 2000, Australia
100 Skyway Avenue, Rexdale, Ontario M9W 3A6, Canada
PO Box 84165, Greenside, 2034 Johannesburg, South Africa
61 Beach Road, Auckland 1, New Zealand

Published by Granada Publishing 1980

ISBN 0 246 11439 8

Text illustrations by Doreen McGuinness of The Garden Studio

Printed in Great Britain by
Richard Clay (The Chaucer Press) Ltd,
Bungay, Suffolk
Phototypesetting by Georgia Origination, Liverpool
Set in Baskerville

For my family

My wife, Elaine,
whose invaluable support brought
The Adventures of Holly Hobbie
to fruition.

My children, Deborah,
Elizabeth, and Daniel.

My sisters, Judy Brown
and Pearl Haimowitz.

My brothers, Dr Alex Dubelman
and Dr Alan Dubelman.

And in loving memory of my parents,
William and Gertrude Dubelman, who taught me
the value of the written word.

ACKNOWLEDGEMENTS

Illustrated by Doreen McGuinness
based on
visuals conceived by Richard Dubelman

Reference and research photography by Elizabeth Dubelman

During research and writing I came across many people who imparted information to me that is incorporated in this novel. Of the people I interviewed and corresponded with, I especially would like to express my appreciation for their generous assistance to Mesoamerican archaeo-astronomer Tony Aveni, Colgate University; Mesoamerican archaeologists Michael D. Coe, Yale University, and William R. Coe, The University Museum, University of Pennsylvania; Gordon Ekholm, American Museum of Natural History; Ian Graham, Peabody Museum, Harvard University; and David Joralemon, Yale University.

I also wish to acknowledge with gratitude the governments of Guatemala and Mexico; my research consultants, Dennis Parrish, Deborah Dubelman, and D. W. Dubelman; and, of course, my native 'bush' guide, Clarence Mossiah.

Note: The word *Maya* refers to the people and the language. *Maya* is also used as an adjective wherever anything pertaining to the Maya is described. Expert archaeologists, anthropologists, and art historians on Mesoamerica who have dealt with the subject and its literature for many years have developed an official policy for the use of the word *Maya* in the nominal, adjectival, and plural forms (and avoid using the word *Mayan*).

The most beautiful experience we can have is the mysterious. It is the fundamental emotion which stands at the cradle of true art and true science.

Albert Einstein,
IDEAS AND OPINIONS

Prologue

July 19

With a staccato popping that seemed totally out of place in the vast stillness, the olive-green Huey helicopter swept low and scudded over the rain forest, heading north in the direction of the Mexican border. Its two occupants intently scanned the monotonous green carpet of forest below. One wore the faded fatigues of a Guatemalan army pilot. The other was dressed in casual civilian clothes suitable for the uncommon July heat.

Enrique Lara did not relish such duty. The emptiness of the Petén jungle always made him uneasy. If anything at all unexpected happened up here, the chances for survival were slim, and even if one survived, it was not a good place to be. He, more than most, knew the routine and the futility of jungle searches by helicopter—and this one was no different from all the others. Suddenly he missed the *cantina* in Flores and the genial smiles and banter of the 'serving girls'. He would even settle for a few rounds of that dreadful warm beer at the military base in Poptún and the companionship of his fellow soldiers.

'It is of no use, Felipe,' he spoke loudly in order to be heard. 'We must turn back soon anyway, or we won't be able to get back to Tikal, much less Flores.'

Felipe Sánchez's tan baseball cap was stained with perspiration, as was his yellow shirt. The large folded map lay in his lap like a used towel. He glanced at it despondently. Not even the black square, the symbol for a single hut, marked its trackless uniformity—only brown contour lines and the occasional fine blue of a stream. Felipe, too, was beginning to wish he were not in this forsaken place. But he couldn't give up yet. 'Let's try one last run.'

The jungle was now interrupted sporadically by patches of tall grass. Ahead, on the left, the late sun caught a glint of water.

'A tributary of the Río Azul,' Felipe noted, pointing to the map. 'Señor Dutton probably would not have gone *this* far. There don't seem to be any ruins near here anyway. We might as well turn back.'

They were over the stream. Enrique turned to follow it briefly before heading south again. In the tangle of shoreline forest there was nothing. Suddenly the dark foliage of a giant ceiba tree exploded in a blaze of red and yellow as a flock of macaws, alarmed by the unaccustomed noise, took to flight. Beside the river two huge logs moved. Alligators. They turned sluggishly, then slithered into the muddy water with hardly a ripple as the Huey passed.

'Look!' The pilot pointed south to the edge of a grassy plain that lay just ahead. He lowered the craft.

In the distance three tiny deer scattered in panic, but their directions were somehow not quite right. Something other than the helicopter had scared them—and very badly.

'*Un tigre!*' Felipe had seen it too.

The grizzled jaguar—a bright spot of yellow against the browns and greens below—bounded gracefully across the clearing in pursuit of one of the deer. Quickly and neatly he pawed his quarry down, and with one bone-crunching bite, death came instantly. Only then did the great beast pause to gaze calmly upward at the machine that had invaded his world.

As Enrique and Felipe craned backward for one final look, the big cat was dragging his victim, jerking but quite dead, into the forest shadows.

'A very dangerous place, *verdad*?' Felipe said.

'Right you are, *compañero*, but not to our boss, Señor Dutton. It is almost good that we have to return now. Bad country.' Then, noticing the look of despair on Felipe's face, Enrique continued, 'It's true that we have found no sign of him. But he knows this country as well as anyone, and he is brave. We will find him one day. Now, though, our fuel is low. I will head us straight for Tikal.'

Lulled by the monotony of the landscape that unrolled below them, neither Enrique nor Felipe paid any particular attention to the low ridge of forest ahead.

The tall, heavily bearded man followed the narrow over-grown trail that skirted the near base of the ridge. His steps were sure, for he knew the jungle as well as any *chiclero*—one of that special tough breed of men hired to roam the forest, slashing the sapodilla trees to collect gray gummy chicle. Archaeologist Mel Dutton had spent much of his adult life in such places, but this was his hardest task—his search for the lost city. In the deep shade of the forest canopy he took off his floppy straw hat and swiped at the clouds of whining mosquitoes, although he had long ago become immune to their bites. He moved quietly along the narrow overgrown trail, pausing now and then to step cautiously over a rotten log or to skilfully wield his sharp Collins machete against the thick vines that hung low over the path. He was surrounded by dense vegetation and some of the most hostile terrain in the world. So intently did he concentrate on his walk now that he seemed

13

scarcely to notice the brief crescendo of the helicopter as it passed above him.

The helicopter approached Tikal, the ancient Maya ruin that lies like a bird's nest surrounded by dense wild green jungle that stretches unbroken to every horizon. As the craft lowered toward the airstrip, the tops of the tall stone temples nearby seemed to rise higher and higher. Still a miraculous city, thought Felipe, even after a thousand years. And somehow forbidding.

Wednesday, November 22

***L**iz* Dutton was slumped
down in her seat, strands of long brown hair strewn across her
strong-featured face. Her bony knees were propped up against
the seat in front of her, and her chin was digging into her chest.
She was pretending to be asleep. The bus had become very
quiet. She listened to the steady hum of the motor and the rhyth-
mic, almost hypnotic, slap of the windshield wipers. '*Dut*-ton, *dut*-
ton *dut*-ton, *dut*-ton,' they seemed to say in a prolonged, ghostly
whisper. It had been raining steadily since she and her brother
had left New York, and the fog was closing in. The huge tyres
made a noise like ripping silk on the smooth pavement of
Interstate 86. Cautiously Liz opened her eyes. The hissing rain
had changed to silent snow, falling in eerie-coloured flakes as
she watched through the heavily tinted bus windows. Then,
just as she was about to close her eyes again, the bus driver
switched on the high beams, and a sign came looming out of
the fog: STURBRIDGE—12 MILES. They were almost there. Liz
had an uncomfortable feeling that someone was watching her.
Turning her head, she saw her brother leaning towards her. He

15

was propping his chin up with a thumb tilting his head high like a professor.

'Boy, Liz, you're really something!'

Liz gave her eleven-year-old brother a withering glance and burrowed down even deeper in her seat, but Danny was not about to be ignored any longer. With a determined smile he passed her the tuna-salad sandwich he had been munching on. Liz refused the offering and picked up the macramé plant hanger she was making for her grandmother.

' "Dear Abby," ' Danny recited mockingly in his best little girl's voice. ' "My father disappeared in a jungle in Guatemala. For a little while they searched. Now even Mum says we have to think of him as dead. You see, I have these dreams..." Where did you ever get the idea of writing *her*?'

Liz jabbed a sharp elbow into Danny's ribs. 'Cool it, you little smart-ass.'

He ignored her. ' "Dear Ms. L. D.," ' he went on, switching to a deeper, teacher-like voice, ' "understanding grown-ups, especially parents, can sometimes be hard for a child..." '

'At least I've been published, Danny. In a syndicated nationwide column,' Liz said sharply. But she could fight back no longer. 'Oh, Danny. I can't stand it. Dad gone and everybody accepting it.'

Danny stopped his teasing. 'Don't you think I miss him, too? I don't want to believe it any more than you do. And neither does Mom. Why do you think she's working so hard now? It's just to keep her from thinking about him lost in that jungle.'

She was silent for a minute and then, in a much more subdued tone, she asked, 'Danny, do you feel funny?'

'No. Why?'

'Well, I do. Every time we get near Grandpa and Grandma's house, I feel kind of...kind of weird.' Her big-sister tone had disappeared. 'I wish Mum didn't have to go to the publishing convention...'

Danny interrupted. 'Don't forget to give Grandpa the new book that Mum edited and tell him it won't be out until spring.'

16

He turned to the window wearily, and Liz sighed with resignation. No one wanted to listen to anything she had to say anymore. Even Mum, who had always said that Liz was more mature and sensible than many of the people she had to deal with daily in her publishing job, had started treating her like a little kid. Now that she was thirteen and her mother needed her more than ever, all her mother seemed to care about was that Liz was *now* failing history and Spanish.

Liz decided to try once more. Danny was always very logical for a kid his age, if she could just manage to get his attention. 'Danny, think about it, this is the twentieth century. He's got to be alive! People don't just disappear, never to be found. It's too horrific!'

Danny winced. 'Where did you pick up such a dismal expression?'

'At school. Everybody says it.'

'Your school is a menagerie. No wonder.'

Liz was about to persist, but at that moment the bus slowed cautiously and swung off the interstate onto the exit ramp. The inside lights dimmed for a second, giving the weary passengers a glimpse of the sparkling white landscape outside.

'Hey, look at that!' Danny murmured and turned to Liz. 'The radio said six inches of snow, and it was right for a change.'

Soon the bus was gliding down the main street of Sturbridge. In the darkness the street lights refracted cheerfully through the bright glow of falling snow. The main part of town dropped behind them as the large vehicle slowed and gently edged to a stop on a lonely country road. The brakes hissed loudly, the wheels stopped, and the snow-covered hulk slid briefly on the slick pavement and bumped against a hardened snow-bank.

'Ol' Sturbridge Village,' announced the driver as the doors swung open and cold fresh air surrounded the weary passengers. Two elderly people were silhouetted against a hardened snowbank.

'We're here, Liz,' Danny reminded his sister. 'Time to smile.'

17

The two gathered their baggage—Liz's blue backpack and Danny's gray canvas carry bag—crowded into the aisle past the other passengers, stepped down, entering the cold, and into the arms of their grandparents.

'Hi, Grandpa, Grandma,' Danny said cheerily while trying to avoid a kiss. 'Greetings from the New York.' Determined not to let his sister's mood spoil the reunion, he continued to chatter. 'Can't wait for skiing—I see you arranged to have snow just for me, and powder, too—perfect for downhill or even cross-country with you, Grandpa.' He looked up, grinning. 'How considerate.'

Agatha and John Dutton smiled at their grandchildren. 'Welcome, sprouts,' John Dutton said. 'You must be tired. Let's get warm.' They all climbed into the old maroon Chevrolet Woodie.

'Actually, Danny,' John Dutton continued as he carefully guided the station wagon down the road toward the house, 'this is just some fake snow I arranged to impress you—just like we used in the movies in the old days. It was really quite warm today, and I thought you'd be disappointed.' The ancient Woodie bounced precariously over the darkened road, weaving its way past the old historical village.

'Oh, John,' chided Agatha from the back seat. 'I'm sure Danny will hear enough of your stories before the holiday is over. Pay more attention to the road.' She turned to Liz. 'Y'know what keeps our marriage going?'

'What's that,' interrupted Danny, finding an opportunity to play straight man.

'I asked your grandfather a simple question forty-five years ago...and he hasn't stopped answering me yet.' The old actor smiled gently, patted Danny on the knee, and said, 'Grandma's acupuncture treatment—ouch! She's always needling me.'

They came to a jolting halt in front of the shadow-mottled old 'Dutton' colonial farmhouse with its dark clapboard facade. By now Liz was beginning to feel more relaxed.

'You'll sleep well tonight, and I'll fix you the best breakfast you ever tasted,' Agatha said, winking.

To which John added, 'You can order anything you want—pancakes, sausage, French toast—or even one of my favourites, plain ol' cornflakes.'

'Y'know grandpa loves cornflakes, 'cause when he chews them, he hears a sound that reminds him of applause.' She chuckled. 'And remember, kids. No school. You don't have to get up tomorrow till you want to.'

Liz leaned over and kissed her grandmother lovingly. 'We're really glad to be here. I want you to know that.'

It was a great wooden place originally built sometime in the early 1700s, but successive additions had long ago distorted the simplicity of the original plan. The old farmhouse appeared serene. Grandma had left the lights burning in the front, and the bright yellow glow could be seen behind the old glass in the small window panels. The house had been the real anchor of the Dutton family. Agatha had moved into the family house shortly after she and John married, and they had kept it through all the years that John travelled, doing the character parts he was famous for. After his acting days he and his wife had returned. Liz and Danny's father had grown up in the house as well, and he had often said—Liz remembered with a pang of loneliness—that someday he, too, would retire to the old place.

Grandpa stopped the wagon in front of the outbuilding that had been converted to a garage of sorts, and the group piled out and entered the warmth of the house with Melissa. The springer spaniel's whole body wiggled with joy. She almost trampled Nehemiah, the orange and white striped cat, in her efforts to welcome Danny and Liz. Danny threw his bag on the floor and knelt to rumple the pendulous ears of his brown and white friend.

'Hi, Melissa,' he greeted. 'You gonna come skiing with me tomorrow?'

They were in the 'new' part of the house, as it was still called, though it had been built in 1850. It was there that John and Agatha Dutton spent most of their time. The oldest section of the house, adjoining, held two floors. It often served as a

19

living history lesson for tourists, particularly the old-fashioned kitchen with its wide plank oak floors and giant fireplace. Agatha even ran a summer antique fair in the barn and gave lectures to people interested in restoring old homes.

For Liz the oldest part was the very soul of the house, for it was where her father's room had been.

The animals followed along as Grandma hurried them past the darkened wing of the house and into the living room. 'I've made up your usual rooms upstairs. It's getting late. Why don't you go up and get ready for bed, and I'll bring each of you a nice cup of hot cocoa to help you sleep.'

After hearing Nehemiah's repeated meows for attention, Liz patted her chest and the cat jumped up at the signal. Liz caught her friend in midair and draped the tiger cat across her left shoulder. Liz felt wide awake, but she wasn't in the mood for talking either, so she grabbed her backpack and headed straight for the stairs. 'I think I'll skip the cocoa, Grandma,' she said brusquely. When she saw the worried look on her grandmother's face, she thought up an excuse. 'It's bad for my complexion,' she added and disappeared upstairs.

'It's bad for my complexion,' Danny mimicked under his breath as he followed her up the stairs. 'Look at me,' he added, posing dramatically in the well of the light at the top of the stairs, 'the skin you love to touch.'

'Enough, Danny. Off to bed with you,' Grandma scolded lightly. Danny quickly countered, 'Why? Isn't there a law against compulsory retirement?'

Liz put Nehemiah on her bed, placed her pack on the ladder-backed chair, and studied her face in a colonial pine bureau mirror. It showed her unhappiness. Nothing seemed right anymore. She was growing up too fast—up, not out. She was failing Spanish and history even worse than her mother knew. Her friends at school didn't seem to want to hang around her anymore and she couldn't blame them. She just wasn't fun. How could she be with those strange nightmares every night.

Close to tears Liz fished a balled-up pair of pajamas from the depth of her pack, put them on, and jumped into the enormous four-poster bed, arranging her legs carefully so as not to disturb Nehemiah. She had slept in this room every time she visited her grandparents since she was a small child, and it had never occurred to her to be afraid until the past summer when she and Danny had stayed at Sturbridge while her mother was in Guatemala, taking part in the search for Dad.

Liz shuddered as she remembered waking up in the middle of the night and noticing a strange sweet smell, like incense wafting through the room. The next morning, when she mentioned it at breakfast, her grandmother denied using incense—hated the stuff, she said. Grandma was sure that Liz had smelled the cleaning wax she used on the antique and fruitwood furniture. But it still didn't explain her strange feeling.

Tonight Liz was not at all sure. She hadn't noticed any furniture-wax smell when she entered the room, but now, as she closed her eyes, the room seemed filled with the familiar heavy odour.

Outside the wind had increased. Liz pulled the Dutch-doll quilt up to her chin and clamped her eyes shut. The wind rose to a long howling whine, then gradually slipped into a low, prolonged moan as if something not human were trying to communicate with her. A large limb on an old oak just outside the window broke with a sharp crack, and a hundred small branches raked their black icy fingers heavily down the side of the house as it fell.

Liz got up and wrapped herself in the quilt from the bed. Something doesn't want me here, she thought. The antique candlestick on the bed table held a fresh candle and a tiny box of safety matches. Liz lit the candle and carried it gingerly into the hall. The house was dark and silent. She made her way carefully downstairs to the living room couch, with Nehemiah following silently alongside, his fur glistening in the candlelight.

'Nehemiah,' she said softly. 'No one believes me. But there's definitely something spooky going on in this house. You know it, don't you?' The cat looked knowingly straight up at Liz.

21

She pulled the quilt snugly around her and began to relax as one finger idly traced the outline of a doll on a square of the quilt—a doll with short, stubby arms, a full old-fashioned blue bonnet, flaring dress of calico and gingham, and black sensible shoes.

Liz blew out the candle, turned on a reading lamp, and grabbed a *National Geographic* from the coffee table to avoid sleep and the terror of that recurring nightmare. How she wished her mother were here.

Hours passed before she felt calm enough to sleep, and when she did drop off, the light burned in the dark room all night. Nehemiah lay at her feet, his paws folded beneath him, and watched Liz, his green eyes focused on her face.

In the Pump Room of the Ambassador East Hotel in Chicago, Elaine Dutton, executive editor of Reynolds Publishing, was about to begin her after-dinner talk before the American Publisher's Association. A sizable audience of writers, agents, editors, and publishers had gathered.

She surveyed her audience calmly, her honey-coloured hair pulled into a soft chignon. She wore a simply cut but elegant tweed suit.

'Writers experience problems we ordinary mortals can only imagine. For example, Mark Twain wrote in bed but gave it up because he claimed the ink dripped all over him.' A titter played across the audience. 'When someone asked E. M. Forster why he hadn't finished a novel in twenty years, he explained that he had sent his characters off on various trains and couldn't figure out how to get them back again.' The crowd warmed with laughter. 'The critics praised Henry James for his compelling portrayal of a neurotic governess haunted by two dead children who exist only as a projection of her own tortured mind, yet as far as James was concerned, *The Turn of the Screw* was a simple ghost story!

'The moral usually drawn from this anecdote is that authors are often the last people to know what their own books are about.' Elaine Dutton paused significantly before continuing.

'But I think we can learn something else from this tale. Most of us have become so used to dealing with the occult as a genre that we often forget that many people, including some quite intelligent people, take the supernatural seriously. My husband, who has spent several years studying the were-jaguar, a common figure in the ancient Olmec art of Mexico, found that many Maya still believe that *shamans*, or priests, can transform themselves into jaguars and thus become were-jaguars.

'When we at Reynolds were considering publishing our first novel on an occult theme, I must admit I took a rather negative view. I thought the occult was beneath our dignity. Then my husband confessed at an Explorer's Club convention that he had once consulted a *shaman* in the Yucatán for help in locating a particularly elusive site. He was convinced that the *shaman* had helped him. So I figured if this stuff is good enough for Henry James and my own husband, it's good enough for me.'

Elaine delivered the line with the timing of an experienced speechmaker and waited for the laughter to die out. Some of the people in the audience noticed that she still referred to Mel Dutton as if he were alive.

'So, I'd *like* to tell you that the decision to publish our best-selling Hathaway's *The Ogilvy Chronicles* was the result of my great literary acumen and our fantastic market research organisation. But it was neither. I'm afraid I still don't believe in ghosts, were-jaguars, ancestral spirits, and ESP. But I do have faith in hunches and instinct.'

Thursday, November 23,
Thanksgiving Day

Outside the snow had stopped, and the light was turning an icy blue. Distorted shadow patterns twirled across the snow. The horses standing in the barn shivered and occasionally rippled their manes.

The faintest trace of incense still lingered in the air. Am I only imagining it? Liz thought. She opened the window. Suddenly she felt a blast of cold, dank air. The north wind chill had eliminated the scent, but even shutting the window again left the room cold. She wrapped her quilt around her shoulders.

Liz remembered the days of waiting for Thanksgiving dinner. There was a time when the very prospect would find her hugging herself in anticipation. Yet this Thanksgiving morning she stood at the living room window as if in a dream. Through the frost on the pane she imagined figures in the snow—herself, Danny, and their parents—as they were years ago.

Dad carried little Danny on his shoulders as Mum and Liz put the finishing touches to a snowman. With its sunken eyes and its black coal mouth slightly downturned, the snowman seemed sad and vulnerable.

24

'The poor snowman is freezing,' Elaine laughed.

'Liz, it's beautiful,' said Mel. 'You've done a terrific job. Look at the noble expression on that face.'

'Can we save him, Daddy?' Liz cried.

'Sure. He's worth immortalizing.'

'Can we put him in the 'frigerator? Can we? Can we make him last forever?'

'For-ev-er?'

Agatha's voice snapped her back to reality.

'Liz! What are you doing up so early. And why is your quilt down here?'.

Liz turned to her grandmother and ran into her arms.

When she was little, Liz had loved exploring the old colonial farmhouse, imagining that there must be secret messages hidden in some nook or cranny by a child who lived here long ago. But today she didn't want to wander around it, didn't even want to join Danny and her grandfather in their cross-country skiing. She watched silently as they set off with Melissa beside them, her paws making their own path through the snow, her nose buried in the drifts. This was the first year Liz hadn't brought any of her friends to Sturbridge for the weekend. It was such fun to show off the farm, the village, and her grandparents—Grandma's special chestnut stuffing, Grandpa's jokes—everything.

But this time Liz felt something eerie about the house. Maybe it was Grandma and Grandpa's insistence on treating every part of the Thanksgiving celebration as they had before Dad's disappearance.

She wanted to talk to her grandmother about it, but she knew how busy Agatha was. She trailed her grandmother silently from room to room, helping to set the table and make the beds, but so lacking was her usual animation that her grandmother finally said, 'I really don't need any more help. Why don't you go out and get some fresh air?'

Liz smiled and said, 'Maybe I should do some homework and fool Mum.'

And before her surprised grandmother could answer, she had once again retreated to her room. But when Nehemiah followed her, he found her notebook closed and Liz crying quietly. He jumped on her lap and arranged his chin carefully over her left arm. She hugged him for comfort.

By four that afternoon Liz, Danny, and Grandma were seated at the dining table, passing steaming bowls of food—tiny green peas, pearl onions in creamy golden sauce, fluffy potatoes, and Grandma's own pickles and cranberry sauce—while Grandpa carved the turkey, roasted to a rich brown crisp and filled with chestnut stuffing.

Grandpa insisted on telling all of his favourite old theater stories, even though Liz and Danny knew them by heart and there were no new friends to hear them this time.

'. . . and the moral is,' Grandpa said with a wave of his hand, 'never go on stage without your belt!'

Danny, concentrating on his food, seemed oblivious to everything. Liz had trouble swallowing. It's just like playacting, she thought. I know the food is good, but it tastes like cardboard.

Still, when the rising tones of Grandpa's voice indicated that he was coming to the end of a story, she made an effort to smile.

Why doesn't he say something about Dad's disappearance? Liz wondered. Maybe he thinks I'm still too young to understand.

After the dinner dishes were washed, Grandma suggested that Liz might like to take a look around the old colonial kitchen. Thinking that now that the chores were over, this would be a good time to talk to Grandma alone, Liz agreed. The old kitchen, which was shut off from the rest of the house in order to save heat, was even colder than the other rooms. Grandma, who always said that city people kept their houses much too warm, didn't seem to be bothered by the chill, but even with a warm wool shawl wrapped around her, Liz could hardly keep her teeth from chattering.

'The whole family once lived in this room' Grandma said proudly. 'See, people didn't have stoves or central heating in

26

those days—the fireplace made do for everything. And look at this rocking chair, it's over two hundred years old. Made by one of your ancestors with his own hands.'

'Why don't you use this room anymore?'

'Oh, honey, it's just too impractical,' said Grandma, blowing dust off the mantel. 'Just a second. Long as we're here, I might as well fetch a duster.'

Left alone, Liz found her attention drawn to a curious old jar with a heavy sort of wooden paddle inside. As she picked it up to examine it, a heavy creaking noise behind her nearly made her jump out of her skin. Flustered, Liz dropped her shawl.

'Did that sound throw a scare into you? Poor dear,' said Grandma, returning to the room just in time to see the shawl slip off Liz's shoulders. It's only the floorboards settling, of course, though your father always did say there were ghosts in this kitchen.' Realising her mistake in mentioning Melville Dutton, Grandma quickly changed the subject. 'Here, let me hold this for you. It's an old eggbeater, you know. What those women must have gone through trying to keep house...'

'Grandma, I want to look at Dad's old room. I haven't been up there for so long.'

'But I promised your mother...well, all right. I don't see any harm in it. Let's go upstairs.'

Liz knew that the small room above the old kitchen had been one of her father's favourite places in the whole world. Even when the whole family came back to Sturbridge for visits, Dad always used this room for his study. Nor would he let Grandma throw away any of his old possessions. The room was crowded but very neat.

An old blackened fireplace, with newly cut logs carefully stacked within, centred the panelled wall opposite th window. The low bookcases on either side of it were filled with the volumes that Mel Dutton had accumulated throughout his school days. A black and gold model ship in full sail stood on top of one; a glass frame of stone arrowheads, wired to a blue velvet background, leaned on the other. The large desk under the window held a china coffee mug full of pens and pencils. Amid the rest of the desk clutter Liz noticed the antique box that held her Dad's drafting instruments. It was open near the stack of small notebooks beside the green blotter. The sturdy captain's chair was pushed at an angle, just as if Mel Dutton had stepped out of the room for a moment. If only that were true, Liz thought with a pang.

'You might like to read some of these old books, dear,' Grandma said, taking Liz by the shoulders and gently turning her away from the desk. 'There are some things here that your father used to read over and over again, like these books by Gann—Thomas Gann, I think, and this one, *The Ancient Maya,* that Morley wrote. Ah, and Stephens!' Agatha recalled, bending to retrieve two antique brown-and-gold volumes from the shelf. 'Your grandfather used to call Mr Stephens "the competition," because one summer your dad was so engrossed in these that he could never seem to find time to do his chores. These are what really made your father decide to become an archaeologist, instead of a doctor, like Grandpa always wanted. I remember John—your Grandpa, I mean—telling Mel that an archaeologist couldn't even make as good a living as an actor.'

'Tell me about these people again, Grandma,' said Liz, pointing to the row of framed portraits on the wall over the bed. 'It's been so long, I've forgotten.'

'Oh, your ancestors. Mel used to love to collect all the old family stuff. Like your Grandpa and me, he always cared about his family roots. People used to think it was a very strange interest for a young fellow. Now, of course, everyone does it. Mel used to say that he liked the idea that they were up there on the wall watching him while he wrote his books. A funny notion...'

'Is *that* one of my ancestors?' Liz asked, pointing to one framed portrait. 'He's really handsome.'

'Oh, yes. That's Lieutenant Cal Dutton of the Ninth Massachusetts Regiment. He was missing in action after the Battle of Vicksburg.'

'You mean he died?'

'Fortunately not. He turned up alive, else where would this family be now?'

28

'So everyone thought he was missing for good, but he wasn't. He came back home,' said Liz, half to herself.

'This is still my favourite picture of your dad,' Grandma said, looking toward a framed cover of *People* that showed a handsome man in mountaineering gear standing on the edge of what appeared to be a precipitous cliff. 'Melville Dutton. One professor who is seldom in class!' the headline trumpeted.

'Really! Doesn't Dad look great there? He kept saying it was all hype, of course. He just did it to help raise money for his next expedition. But I thought the article was really good. Daddy *is* brave, like the old-time explorers.'

'Liz, dear, look at this one,' said Grandma, pointing to the largest oil portrait, framed in gold next to a yellowing scrap of stitched sampler bearing the phrase, 'In the Darkness of the Night, Courage Always Finds the Light.'

'Your dad always called that picture "Old Aunt Holly." She was supposed to have done that sampler herself.'

The painting showed a girl maybe slightly older than Liz. She was in a full simple dress of calico and gingham, with an apron over it. In the three-quarter view a blue calico bonnet and a heavy shadow hid most of the face, but the few wisps of redddish-brown hair that showed along the slender cheek and down her back emphasized her breathtaking beauty. The steady gaze of a confident and slightly prim brown eye was softened by the trace of an impish smile.

' "Old Aunt Holly"? But she doesn't look old...'

'That's a picture of her when she was a little girl about your age,' Grandma said with a smile. 'They say she came from right here in Sturbridge Village, almost two hundred years ago, and lived pretty much the way they show things in the living museum of Old Sturbridge Village now.'

'But what was she like? And who were her parents? Did she farm like Grandpa does now? Did she go to school?'

'They say Holly was well read and schooled in all the graces of her day. She studied the classics in Latin and Greek and spoke several other languages. She also played the pianoforte, an old-style piano. Her family? Well, according to best recollections on the subject, her mother's ancestors came over

29

on the Mayflower. Of course the name "Hobbie" doesn't appear in the Mayflower log because it would have been her mother's family name that was listed and nobody seems to remember it for sure.'

'But where did this painting come from?'

'It was done in 1803, during Thomas Jefferson's presidency, by a man named Nigel Kirkwood, of the Gilbert Stuart school of art. Everyone who's seen it feels there's *something* special about it... not just paint on canvas.'

'You can feel the vibes,' Liz said. 'It's almost like it has a special life of its own. Maybe it's because there's such a brightness in her eyes.'

'Holly's father is supposed to have believed the portrait had a certain 'indefinable magic.' I don't know about that,' Grandma went on, 'but it certainly glows with a spiritual expression, and there's a different look and mood to it every time you see it. I guess maybe it depends on the quality of light in the room. Though Mr Kirkwood himself wrote that on at least one occasion the girl in the portrait had definitely *shifted* her position.'

'Far out, Grandma. Do you believe in miracles like that?'

'Well, I don't know about miracles. I just know that some things are too complicated to be readily understood. Maybe, as one philosopher said, miracles are just propitious accidents. Y'know, in addition to being a distinguished artist, Nigel Kirkwood was also known at the local pubs as a gregarious raconteur, a great storyteller. Anyway, I like having Holly in this room. She gives it a special combination of young yet old-world wisdom. Your father used to feel he could learn about the family from her. He was fascinated, you know, by how people today became the way they are. He liked to think that by understanding things like Holly's old world and the mystery of the Maya civilization, we could learn more about ourselves.' She stopped herself. 'I promised I wouldn't dwell on your father this weekend.'

'But I want to talk about him.'

'No more tonight. You still look so tired, Liz. Do you want to go to bed early again?'

'Maybe I will. But can I sleep up here tonight, Grandma? Please?'

'Well, I suppose so...why not? I'll make up a fire, and you get your things.'

Twenty minutes later Liz was in her pyjamas, trying not to look impatient as Grandma finished, positioning the back log, stoking the fire, and saying good night. As soon as she heard the sound of Grandma's footsteps reach the bottom of the stairs, Liz jumped out of bed and began rifling through her father's desk. The first thing she found was an old green photograph album, its cover labelled: Family: 1965-1970. Here would be her early childhood—she and her parents in much happier times.

Quickly Liz pulled the soft down comforter off the bed and curled up near the firelight to peruse the album. Before she realized it, the fire was nearly out, and Liz had to squint to see the dim pictures.

Danny, Liz mused to herself. I ought to show this to Danny. On second thought, she realized, he won't pay any attention. Once Danny decides I'm being emotional, there's no talking to him.

Liz crawled into bed. Feeling utterly miserable and alone, even with Nehemiah in a ball at her feet, she cried quietly into the pillow until she couldn't fight sleep and began to drift off.

'Liz, honey, look at this one,' the voice said. It was Daddy! Liz found herself crawling laboriously up a trail strewn with giant boulders. She knew from the heavy feeling in her arms and legs that she must be dreaming, but the scene seemed so real. She and her dad used to climb this trail on the Palisades, just across from New York, almost every Saturday during the summers, when Dad was home from the field.

'Dad, don't get so far ahead,' Liz heard herself scream. 'I couldn't see where you were.'

'Did you think I'd disappear, sweetheart? Come on, you know better than that. Now take a look at this. These Palisades are some of the hardest rock layers in the world.'

Liz sat up in bed, wide awake. The voice could have been right in the room with her.

I've been listening to too much of Danny's junk about ESP, Liz thought. How any kid who thinks so highly of science can be interested in that stuff is beyond me.

31

Her eyes fell on the big portrait of 'Old Aunt Holly.' The surface of the painting caught the last flickers of the dying fire in an uncanny half-light that also played over Liz's face.

'In the darkness of the night,' she intoned, half to herself, 'courage always finds the light. . . I wonder if Aunt Holly really believed that.'

Liz, very tired now, began tossing and turning restlessly, trying desperately to stay awake and thus avoid entering the dark world of her recurring nightmare. She knew it all too well. The pictures of terror would begin to form in her mind and begin to move. Always the same.

A black jaguar and a spotted jaguar raced towards her in slow motion, every sinew and muscles straining. Now she began to fall, and the huge round face of her Spanish teacher appeared.

'Study, Señorita Dutton. Es muy fácil, muy fácil to find your father.'

All around her parrots shrieked, 'El tigre, el tigre!' as the monkeys playfully teased her. Up ahead in the shadowed clearing under a tree, her dad appeared. Although he looked straight at her, he could not see her. The gigantic cats began to circle her father.

'Daddy, Daddy!' she called. The cats circled him now as he knelt to study an ancient round stone altar carved with the face and paws of a jaguar and the body of a man—the were-jaguar. Closer and closer the cats came to her unsuspecting father.

Liz's feeling of helplessness became physical paralysis. She watched her father's body writhe in pain, and she was unable to scream or move to help him.

She would awaken, soaked with perspiration, her pulsebeat accelerated enormously.

No, she couldn't go to sleep and risk that dream again.

A log shifted in the fireplace and a shower of sparks briefly illuminated the room, casting long shadows over the ancient polished planks of the floor. The whole room seemed to glow with haloes of unbearably bright light, for Liz could see no shadows in this bleached room. She blinked. All went dark again, then the glow came once more. A pencil rolled across the desk top and fell to the floor. Liz blinked again in astonishment, then fear clutched her as she gazed once more at the portrait. The gold frame was still there. And so was the tattered sampler. But the portrait had changed. It *had*. Aunt Holly's eyes now gazed full face into the room as flames danced wildly in the fireplace and heat waves shimmered. Her vision was obscured. Then Liz, coiled in terror beneath the covers, heard it: a girl's voice near her, whispering slowly:

'Odd is the night
About to begin
Colder, much stranger
Than it's ever been.
Danger for you
Brings Holly once more
To help with what's coming
For I've lived here before.'

'Who said that?' Liz managed to say from under the thick quilt.

'I did—Old Aunt Holly, naturally.'

'Shut up. This is a dream...this is a dream...*Please*...this *is a dream*!' cried Liz determinedly, flinging off the thick covering. Nehemiah jumped from the bed and ran to safety under it.

'Maybe you are dreaming, maybe you are not,' the voice continued.

All appeared normal. The remnants of the fire glowed reassuringly; the small ship stood poised at full sail; Lieutenant Dutton glared from beneath his blue officer's cap; and Old Aunt Holly...

It couldn't be, thought Liz, almost absentmindedly. The great frame was still there...the portrait was gone.

Liz closed her eyes tightly, and tears glinted in the firelight. When she opened them again, she raised up on one elbow, ready to bolt from the room. But someone was seated on the end of her bed: a girl about her age, dressed in the same clothing that Old Aunt Holly had been wearing in the portrait! Her skin was a beautiful ivory, her cheeks were apple red, and her hair was the colour of reddish, warm honey. Her eyes were deep and luminous and her soft mouth was set in the framework of a small but determined chin.

'Please stay.'

'What is it? Who are you?'

'Holly Hobbie.'

'Who's that? Grandpa?'

'Holly.'

'Come on, Grandpa.'

'No, it's me . . . Holly . . . Holly Hobbie. Where are you going?'

'I'm *leaving*! Grandpa, if this is you, you finally fooled me. This is the best darned ventriloquist trick you've ever pulled.'

'Wait. How often do you talk with someone from the past?'

The voice couldn't have been Grandpa's, she thought. In fact it had a certain soft melodiousness she'd never heard in *anyone's* voice.

'This is getting too real to be a dream. I can't believe I'm saying this, but . . . are you . . . some kind of ghost?' Liz whispered.

'Touch a ghost, it melts away,' Holly smiled perkily.

Liz sat frozen, stunned, unable to say anything as she stared at the portrait come to life. Everything about Holly was alive and fresh—definitely 'of this world.'

Nehemiah's head appeared from under the bed. The cat seemed to have decided to accept the visitor. He leaped onto the mantel of the fireplace.

Pushing back the covers, Liz got up and, with a slight hesitation, touched Holly. When her fingers felt a cold pewter bracelet, she pulled away, almost as if she had touched something red hot.

The 'ghost' looked disappointed. 'For a person who needs someone in whom to confide, you surely do not offer a warm welcome,' she said. 'Especially to my own room.'

'You mean, this was your *pad?*'

'No,' a confused Holly said while reaching into her carpetbag. 'I keep my writing pad in here!'

Liz collapsed with nervous laughter.

'Trust me, Liz. Believe in me. I am here to be your friend.'

Liz closed her eyes tightly. . . . When she opened them again, she raised up on one elbow, ready to bolt from the room. But someone was seated on the end of her bed: a girl about her age, dressed in the same clothing that Old Aunt Holly had been wearing in the portrait!

'Well, if you're really Holly Hobbie, then where do you come from?'

'For as long as I can recall, my spirit has been inside the portrait, painted of me when I was thirteen. That was in 1803, the second year after Mr Jefferson's inauguration.'

'My grandmother gave me the history lesson,' Liz said. 'I'm a lot more interested in hearing how you got here tonight.'

'As I was about to relate, I have been watching everything that happens in this room ever since my portrait was placed here.'

'You mean, you've been watching *me?*'

Getting up from the edge of the bed, Holly bent forward and wrapped her arms around the back of her legs. Then she started lowering her head to the ground.

'What are you doing?' Liz demanded.

'I need to stretch my body after being confined so long.' She straightened herself and began stretching from side to side. 'This is good for the circulation.'

'Have you ever come back before?'

'No, this is my first excursion out of the picture frame.'

'Why are you appearing to me now?'

'You are the first girl descendant nearly my age who has ever slept in this room.'

'If you're real, then how did you work that trick?' Liz said sceptically. 'Are you an astral projection or an out-of-body experience?'

Holly had completed her exercises. 'I am not acquainted with your terminology. All I know is *you willed me* at the right time. And this room and this house are very special to me. I know no special magic—I was never good at parlour tricks—but I can do one thing to convince you of who I am.I can take you back to my own century to show you how this house once looked. Follow me.'

Liz looked around for Nehemiah, but the cat had disappeared under the bed again, driven there by Holly's calisthenics. Liz grabbed Grandma's old shawl for warmth and followed Holly's path to the stairs' landing. But Holly was nowhere to be seen. From the old kitchen below came the glow of firelight. And she heard the sounds of voices, strange voices that spoke very slowly yet full of life.

'I'm still dreaming,' Liz muttered, trying to convince herself as she tiptoed along down the stairs and peeked around the balustrade into the kitchen. Candlelight gleamed and reflected the pewter objects above the now roaring fireplace.

The room which had been cold and bare earlier that day was now alive with people. There, before the fireplace, stood a woman in a long old-fashioned dress using the same cooking utensils Liz had noticed in her grandmother's kitchen earlier. Hanging from a hook in front of the fireplace was an iron pot. The woman was using a large metal spoon to stir what smelled like a stew. From the baking oven came the odour of bread. There were herbs drying in the rafters. The pewter plates for dinner were warming on the mantel. A springer spaniel stretched out comfortably before the fire. The dog, though unfamiliar to Liz, bore similar markings to Melissa.

Seated on a wooden chair to one side of the woman was a girl who looked just like Holly. Suddenly Liz realized it *was* Holly, writing rhymes on a slate. Liz wondered if these people could see her. She pressed herself into the shadow of the doorway so as to remain unnoticed. Nehemiah startled Liz as he brushed against her.

A baby began to cry.

'Rock your brother, Holly dear, and stop writing all that poetry. You are old enough to know your responsibilities,' Holly's mother said.

Slowly Holly rose, walked over to the old colonial wooden cradle on the other side of the fireplace, and leaned forward and began rocking her baby brother gently.

A young girl about two years older than Holly was busily darning a sock. Hardly looking up she said, 'Your poetry seems much more important to you of late than your housework. You will not be a suitable wife if you continue to neglect your chores for just book learning and other such nonsense.'

Holly, ignoring her sister's comments, turned and faced her mother. 'I can do *more* than you expect and still have time for

37

poetry and music, Mother,' she said confidently. 'You know that Father enjoys listening to me recite. When will he be home?'

'Your father is at the harnessmaker's shop. I expect him shortly. You may set the table now.'

Liz heard the creaking of the floorboards, the same sound that had scared her when she was in the kitchen alone earlier that evening. Turning in the direction of the noise, she saw a man sitting in Grandma's old rocking chair. The man's face was in shadow. He was skimming an old *Gazette* and suddenly announced. 'That scoundrel Napoleon just swindled us by selling us that worthless Louisiana Territory for fifteen million dollars. I always said buying real estate is not a good investment.' No one paid him any attention. So he went back to the story he was telling earlier.

'. . .the moral is, never go to church without your belt!' he said, chuckling to himself.

Liz and Holly regained the hall.

Liz clapped a hand over her mouth, ran back up the stairs, and fell onto the bed, shaking with giggles over the thought of how old her grandfather's joke was.

'Memories are made to share, 'tis quite like really being there,' Holly said. 'I wanted you to have a glimpse of my world. It is important for you. Those who do not study history are doomed to relive it. Now if you still think I do not exist, I shall take my leave.'

'No. No. Please. I don't know who you are, but at least you listen to me.'

'Then tell me. What is it that has been giving you these sleepless nights?'

'It's my dad!'

'I know your father. I have sat in my picture frame and watched him often. I have wondered, I must confess, why young Master Melville has not been back to this room of late.'

'Young Master Melville—I mean Dad—is lost in Central America. Mum says—everybody says—we have to face the fact that he may be dead.'

38

'When death knocks, all men must answer,' Holly intoned soberly.

'Look, knock it off with all those sayings, will you? Anyway, as I was trying to explain, there's no evidence that he's dead. He could be just lost; he could be lying somewhere in the jungle, injured. . .he could need help!'

'It is tragic, I admit. Your fear will not be assuaged easily. Please be calm and let us reason. I know your father quite well. At least I believe I do, since I have known him these many years. He was ever resourceful and never seemed to panic. I remember one evening billows of smoke came from somewhere downstairs. A fire, as best I could tell. Smoke was everywhere. Mel—he was about our age—evidenced no fear. He merely got up, left the room, awakened everyone, and then he came back.'

'Why?' Liz asked.

'To recover some irreplaceable artifacts. Still calm, he also collected a few books and instruments and walked out—walked, mind you—even thinking to close the door behind him! Mel Dutton always had the instinct for survival. Besides, heroism feels and never reasons and therefore is always right.'

'But he could need our help!'

'Has no one gone looking for him?'

'Oh, sure. With planes, helicopters, radar. . .everything.'

'The best work is the work done with thine own hands. That is what I have always heard tell.'

'Exactly, Holly. That's how I'm going to find him.'

'That is the proper attitude, Liz,' Holly agreed enthusiastically 'Is it all right to call you Liz?' she added hesitantly.

'Sure. I guess you've known the family long enough.'

'Well, where is our beginning?'

'I haven't a clue,' replied Liz. 'But I have the last letter I got from Dad—last winter. I'll get it.'

Liz pulled a bulging wallet from a small pocket on the side of her backpack and found a tattered sheet folded carefully in the secret compartment. She opened it and bent closer to the light to read the dim writing:

Near Uaxactún, El Petén,
Guatemala
March 22

Dearest Liz,

Right now I'm sitting on the most comfortable log I've seen in days, and am thinking about home and all of you, so thought I'd take a few moments to write.

The weather is quite hot — much too hot for this time of year, in fact — and the unexpected rains have not helped matters much. We are still exploring the area east of Uaxactún and have made camp for the night in the midst of some old mounds belonging to a site that, so far as I know, doesn't even have a name. Clarence Macomber located another limestone cave in the area, one with some stelae nearby. I owe much to this amazing black man from Belize.

Though he had no formal education, he is by far the best-informed person in these parts, and I sometimes think he would make a better archaeologist than some of my colleagues.

We're on the trail of some new monuments which Sean Wilkins heard about from someone. He didn't say who. Clarence, naturally, knows about them, too, and says he can lead me to them. According to his description, one of them has an earthquake reference and the place name of the ruin I am searching for — so my hopes are high.

Here, for you, is a gift which is very valuable archaeologically. It's a lovely Maya jade that is very old — and I think it relates somehow to my lost city. I call it the Jaguar City, since the name is symbolized by the jaguar head this pendant is carved into, and by another jaguar head engraved on the back:

Take very good care of this, my dear.

The President of Guatemala allowed me to keep it as a reward for my work.

I may not have time to write Herschel Goodman anytime soon. If he should call, just tell him that I'm on my way to Tikal and will write him in detail from there, for I have much to tell him about earthquakes and Venus. That should intrigue him! You might also mention that I am still "jaguar hunting." He'll know what I mean.

Our guides, Jorge and Jesús López, have just come into the camp with a deer they killed on the trail. They're now building a fire in the thatch lean-to, and I must help them. The meal will be welcome, the fire won't! Even Clarence is beginning to notice the heat, though he would never complain. Right now he's trying to get the mold out of my camera lens.

Take care, Liz. I miss you all.
Soon I'll be back, and we can have
your belated birthday party. I will
have to go to the Peabody Museum
to take another look at the monument from Tikal. Give my love
to your Mom and Danny. I will
be writing them soon.

As always,
Dad

'I want to see what he sent you,' cried Holly eagerly. 'Do you have it still?'

'Of course. Dad said to take good care of it, didn't he?'

Liz reached inside her pyjama top and pulled out a shiny green plaque she had been wearing on a leather thong around her neck. It caught briefly against a button, then glistened in the light as Liz turned it in her hand.

'Goodness,' Holly exclaimed. 'It is no wonder you cannot sleep with something that big around your neck—and that ugly. It resembles a heathen idol,' she said quietly, fingering the carving suspiciously.

'You're right in a way. According to the letter Dad sent, it's a carving of the head of a jaguar—a kind of big jungle cat. Dad also mentioned that the Indians sometimes used animal heads like this as symbols in their writing.'

'But what about those other things?' Holly indicated a series of small markings on the back of the object.

'Why, I never really noticed those,' answered Liz, turning the flat jade to see better. 'Look, the light barely catches them. These must have been scratched in with a very thin needle or something. It's all writing like I told you about. Here's the jaguar head again, in these other symbols. What in the world!'

'Since your Dad's letter mentioned "Venus", maybe it is *not* in this world.'

'Oh, hush,' chided Liz, glancing at the letter again. 'I wonder what he's going to the Peabody Museum again for? He was just there last December.'

'Peabody. That's a fine New England family,' Holly said thoughtfully. 'There is even a book in this very room about the Peabodys. I watched your father reading it.' Holly went to the shelf and pulled out a heavy volume entitled, *Masterpieces of the Peabody Museum*. Resisting Liz's attempt to snatch the book from her hands, she sat cross-legged by the fireplace and began flipping through the pages. 'Glory be,' she said. 'It is filled with pictures of demons. And I thought the Peabodys were upright, God-fearing folk.'

'Come on, Holly, let me look at that.' Liz reached over Holly's shoulder and began turning the pages more rapidly. 'There it is! We've found it,' she cried, pointing to a small photograph. ' "Cast of Stela 40, Tikal, Guatemala. Date: circa 633." That's all it says.'

'I am not sure that this means anything,' said Holly. 'But if the Peabodys really do have an idol that was made around 633—that is what "circa" means in Latin, you know—I would certainly wish to see it if I were you.'

'Why not?' cried Liz, surprised by her own daring. 'Why not go to Boston and take a look?'

'Boston? Boston is a three-day journey, that is "why not"!'

Liz looked aghast. 'Holly, we're not living in the Stone Age anymore. We can hitch a ride to Boston and be there in an hour and a half. Boston has changed a lot since you last saw it.'

'I have never been to Boston. Young ladies in my day did not travel much—and not at all on impulsive journeys. Besides, I was always busy with my chores.'

'Well, if you can make an "impulsive journey" all the way to the twentieth century from 1803, you can certainly go as far as Boston. I followed you into the past, Holly. Now you come with me. Trust me. And that will prove you're not just a silly ghost or a figment of my imagination.'

'Put yourself to sleep now, and when you awaken, you will learn whether I am here.'

'Holly, I didn't mean to upset you, it's just that. . .'

'Hush, now.' Holly tucked Liz into bed.

'Sleep tight.' Holly sat with Liz until she was asleep, then wrapped herself in a shawl, settled sedately into the rocker, and gazed into the dying fire.

Tikal, Guatemala
Thursday, November 23

With a swiftness bred of lifelong experience, Feliciana Uc pinched a bit of fine ground tortilla dough from the large batch beside her, made it into a ball, and slapped it onto a square piece of banana leaf. Rotating the leaf on the surface of the low roughhewn table, she deftly flattened the doughball into a thin disk, then whisked the finished tortilla onto the *comal*—a blackened circle of thin metal held over a flowing fire by three large irregular rocks.

Feliciana Uc was a Maya. The fabulous civilization of her ancestors had flourished while Europe was still in the Dark Ages. Now, after four hundred years, the Maya were little more than the stepchildren of conquest; they were still farming and working on the land of the ancients. Feliciana and her husband, Raúl, also a Maya, had come to Guatemala from Yucatán more than twenty years ago. Raúl, a master stonemason, had come to work on the great ruin of Tikal in a remote place in the jungle far from any town like those Feliciana had known.

Even *las ruinas,* the ruins, were different here. The mounds

47

were so much higher, so much steeper than those of faraway Yucatán. Feliciana had looked with apprehension at the giant buildings of Tikal and had joked with Raúl to hide her fear.

'You will try not to fall off one of *these,* my husband,' she had said. 'We would never find you.'

'Do not worry, Feliciana,' he had spoken. 'My work will not be on the great *monticulos.* We will be repairing the smaller buildings at first.'

And so they had. Many archaeologists had come during those years while Raúl worked at Tikal, and the place had become almost a town in itself, with several stores, an improved airfield, and for the tourists even a primitive hotel, the Jungle Inn. Feliciana had worked there briefly, making beds for the *gringos* who came to see the great ruins and wander briefly in the shaded forest that surrounded them. Raúl had liked his work. Not only was he in great demand for the work of restoring the fallen stone walls of the old buildings—but he had learned to dig as well, to cut careful straight trench walls and to clear delicate discoveries like burials without the slightest damage. He had also become good at telling the archaeologists where the tombs would be.

Then the work ended. The archaeologists began leaving Tikal, and only small groups of workers remained—those who had nothing to do but keep the grassy plazas neatly trimmed or to help wandering tourists find their way back to the hotel.

Last winter she and Raúl had begun to speak of returning to Yucatán when suddenly Raúl had got work again. A strange job with Señor Sean Wilkins, who was some kind of archaeologist. They dug in mounds, and they moved from ruin to ruin along the jungle trails. Much of their work seemed to be at night for some reason, and often Raúl and other of Wilkins's men would come before dawn with crates to store behind the house. 'Wilkins will get them out later,' was Raul's answer whenever Feliciana had asked what they had found.

Then Raúl had vanished. He had been gone for almost four months now, and Feliciana was almost overcome by the heavy quiet agony of the wait. At first, only a week after Raúl had failed to come home, she had gone to the camp where Señor

Wilkins stayed when he was at Tikal. He was there, but Raúl was not.

'Raúl?' Wilkins had asked, almost in surprise. 'I have not seen him, Señora Uc—not in two days.' Wilkins was calm and reassuring. 'Doubtless he has gone to Flores. Probably he's in the *cantina* still,' he continued in a feeble attempt at joking.

'Raúl does not drink, Señor Wilkins,' replied Feliciana, her eyes cast to the ground. 'Nor does he go to Flores on his own without telling me. I must find him.'

'Please do not worry,' Wilkins had answered coolly, with a glance at his men. 'Raúl will come back. And if he doesn't soon, we will find him.'

'The helicopter,' Feliciana remembered. Could not the helicopter that is now searching for Professor Dutton look for Raúl as well?'

'Perhaps,' Wilkins had answered, turning away. 'If there is anything we can do for you until he comes, please let me know.'

What do Señor Wilkins or any of them know of the jungle, Feliciana thought scornfully as she finished the last of the tortillas. They even get others to dig for them. Not one of them could find his way to water here without some Maya leading him by the hand. She smiled to herself and picked up the gourdbowl of warm tortillas she had made for the tourists' supper at the Jungle Inn. She bolted the wooden door of the house behind her and quietly moved down the trail toward the hotel.

An hour later Feliciana returned. The fragile paper bag she carried held four gold boxes of English cigarettes and five bottles of beer.

Feliciana set the bag carefully on the low table and lit the kerosene lantern that hung from a hook in the centre of the room. She opened a wicker hamper that stood against the wall and searched through the small pile of white dresses until she found her best *huipil,* embroidered with a wide border of pink and red roses. She had stitched it patiently with her own hands many, many years ago.

Soon dressed, she carefully wrapped the cigarettes and beer

in a cloth, along with a few tortillas. Then she reached into a hole in the thatch just above the top of the pole wall and withdrew a crumpled bag that contained her most precious possession: a small snarling clay head, part of a little jaguar the ancients had made. Raúl had given her the piece after he had come back from one of the mysterious trips with Wilkins. She would take it to the holy man, the priest.

In the dim moonlight the Flores road was a narrow white slash through the dark forest. The side trail to the priest's house lay in almost absolute darkness, but just when Feliciana felt that she could not go another step, she saw a tiny light ahead and smelled copal incense. She stepped into the clearing.

The holy man sat before an altar-platform made of branches bound together with vines. The candles around the altar played a soft glowing light on the trees that ringed the clearing, giving them an appearance of dark brooding giants standing in silent watchfulness. An old, smoke-blackened crucifix dominated the centre of the altar. A ring of gourds surrounded it, each filled with *balche,* the liquor of fermented honey and bark beloved by the god Chaac himself. At the front of the altar, piled on top of an old feed sack, were a profusion of cigarette packs, bottles of soda, and canned goods. Feliciana studied the priest's face and noted with satisfaction that he was very old and very ugly—a good sign.

Respectfully she placed her own gifts among those brought by previous supplicants and stated her business. Choosing her words carefully, Feliciana pleased with the priest to intercede on behalf of a man who had lost his way in the forests. She did not mention Raúl's name—to do so would be risky if there happened to be night spirits close by who might overhear.

Moving with great difficulty, the priest went to the altar, knelt reverently before it, and pulled white lumps of copal incense from a bag that hung from his belt. He tossed the copal onto a flat rock with a dent in its top. His movements became slower, more deliberate. He touched a thin dried branch to a candle and almost as in a dream set fire to the copal. Flecks of ash spiralled upwards in swirls of thick black smoke. The smoke hung suspended in the silent air, its strange and twisted shape directly over the altar.

As Feliciana Uc stood unmoving, the old man began to chant softly, rocking back and forth on his haunches and staring into the copal fire. Then, rising with great difficulty, he bent over the altar, took up one of the gourds of brown liquid and handed it to Feliciana, commanding her to drink it quickly.

The *balche* lit a fire in Feliciana's nearly empty stomach. She leaned against the roots of a breadnut tree to steady herself and noted with alarm that the scene before her had begun to glow with unearthly colours. The priest had begun to circle the clearing. He was moving very fast now, very agilely, and he seemed, to Feliciana's swimming brain, to háve suddenly grown much younger. As she watched in amazement and fear, he darted into the undergrowth and returned carrying a struggling figure.

'It is a child,' Feliciana thought groggily, 'a sacrifice to Chaac and the jaguar spirit, just as in the old days.'

The priest held the struggling body over the altar, blocking it from her with his own body, and intoned a strange chant—a melody Feliciana remembered vaguely from the ceremonies she had witnessed in her childhood long ago. Then with lightning speed he produced a knife from his loincloth and slashed the throat of his struggling victim. Blood spattered over the altar and spilled down onto the pile of bottles and cigarettes below. The priest waved the severed head triumphantly. Feliciana wanted to run away, but her body seemed to have turned to stone. Then her eyes went dark, and she could hear only the wavering voice of the priest, chanting: •

> '*Balam, balam...*
> *Spirit of the Jaguar,*
> *Spare the man who wanders the forests*
> *of the Maya...*
> *Kinich-Aháu, the sun-faced God,*
> *watch over him.*

Spirit of the ceiba, tree of life,
sustain his breath.
Souls of his ancestors,
arise now from sleep
And lead him back to his home fires.
Balam the mighty,
Turn your anger against his enemies.
Make the earth shake with the force
of your anger...'

When Feliciana's sight returned, the priest was seated in his old place as if nothing had happened and flung across the altar was the slaughtered corpse...of a young goat. Feliciana sighed. This was a good priest, very powerful.

'Very soon,' the priest rasped, 'a man who has been lost will be found, and he will be alive and safe. A young girl who died but did not really die will come from the land of the north...the past will become the present...I can see it clearly, but do not understand it well.'

When? thought Feliciana. Where is my husband, Raúl?

'I cannot tell where he is, woman,' the priest said, almost in answer to her thoughts. 'Do not worry.'

'It is good that my husband lives,' Feliciana replied gratefully. She thanked the priest, offered him two crumpled *quetzal* notes in payment for his service, and began the long walk back along the trail to Tikal.

After she had left the clearing, the old man shook his head and spat. Husband, he thought. That could not be the man I saw in the vision. Surely he is not a bearded foreigner, a *gringo*. Wearily he reached for one of the warm beer bottles, pried off the cap with the still bloody edge of his old knife, and took a long drink.

'No matter,' he told himself. 'Feliciana Uc is a good woman with faith in the old ways—and the power of the gods is very strong.'

Daylight sent rose-coloured light across the wide domain of the sun god. The old man gathered up the remains of his sacrificial goat and carried it to the ravine behind his house.

When Liz opened her eyes the morning after Thanksgiving, she found Holly fast asleep beside her on the bed, her slip serving as a nightgown and her shawl as a blanket. So Holly wasn't just another dream. But would she go with Liz to Boston? And how soon could they get started? It wasn't even seven o'clock yet, but she couldn't wait.

Liz jumped out of bed, changed into her jeans and sweater, and began stuffing clothes into her backpack. She wanted to take everything she had with her: there was no telling how long they would be gone. The noise of her movements woke Holly, who sat up in bed, trying to contain a yawn. 'I had forgotten that being corporeal was so fatiguing,' she said.

'Corporal? How did the military get into this? Come on, Holly, hurry up and get dressed. Corporal?'

'Not corporal, corporeal,' Holly chastized. 'I fear your vocabulary is limited. I quite agree, however, about the need for haste. If your grandmother finds one of her paintings passing the time of day about the house, I may never get to see Boston. But tell me, please, where is your pitcher and bowl? I must wash before I dress.'

Liz walked Holly to the bathroom and gave the astonished girl her first lesson in sinks, running water, taps, and toilets. 'All of this was in the next room to me all of this time?' Holly asked, amazed.

When Holly returned, her face scrubbed and shining, her eyes still wide with the miracle of a bathroom, she began the elaborate process of getting into her clothes: patchwork dress, long white stockings, high leather shoes. With only a slight glance at the mirror, she shook her copper hair and let it fall into place.

Holly noticed Liz stuffing clothes into her backpack. 'Why are you putting together so many belongings?' she asked. 'You said yourself this is a short journey we are taking.'

'I just want to be ready in case we have to go on from there. Dad taught me to think ahead.'

'Then I shall carry my bag, too.' She held up her carpetbag.

'Where did that come from, anyway?' Liz asked. 'You didn't have it when you were in the frame.'

'It was on the floor beside my feet, and so you could not see it in the portrait.'

'But what's in it except your pad?' Liz smiled at the memory. 'You don't have any other clothes with you, do you?'

'It contains some change of clothes, a fresh apron, some clean stockings and handkerchiefs. . .anything I really need.'

Liz was impressed. 'I thought I got along on a little. But okay, Holly, you pack up and then slip downstairs and wait behind the old woodshed. That way you won't be seen from my grandparents' windows. Meanwhile I'll get on my boots and ski jacket and go wake Danny and try to convince him to come with us. Danny's a bug on parapsychology. He'll believe in you even though he doesn't believe a word *I* tell him.'

Liz gave Holly plenty of time to get safely out of the house. Then, as quietly as possible, she opened the low, narrow door that led from the hall outside the bedroom into the newer wing of the house. Fortunately the door to her grandparents' room was shut tight, and she was able to make her way down the long hall and into Danny's bedroom without stepping on a single creaky floorboard.

Danny was all curled up under the covers. Liz poked at him impatiently. 'Danny! Wake up!'

Still asleep, Danny mumbled, 'Don't make me bunt, coach. I can hit Seaver with my eyes closed.'

'Danny, puh-*leeze* wake up! It's important!'

Danny opened his eyes tentatively and groaned. 'What?...What is it?...What's the matter, can't you see I'm playing for the Yankees? It's my turn to hit!'

'Danny, listen to me! Last night, up in Dad's room, something very remarkable happened, and I discovered...'

Danny rubbed his bleary eyes. 'You're daydreaming again,' he said as Liz raced on in a frenzy.

'Look, I can't explain it all now, but I met someone from the past, a friend, one of our ancestors. We were looking at the thing Dad sent me—the stone carving I wear—and we found another picture of it, at least we're pretty sure it is, in a book about the Peabody Museum so tell Grandma and Grandpa not to worry because we went off to Boston and do you wanna come too?'

'Come where? Ancestor? Who's we?'

'To Boston...with me and Holly Hobbie. It's hard to explain, but you see she wants to help me because she's my friend and after all he's her relative too!'

Whose?' blurted Danny, totally bewildered.

'Dad's! Haven't you heard a word I've said?'

Danny looked at the clock on his bedside table and shuddered. 'If you're going to Boston with some strange relative when it's still the middle of the night as far as I'm concerned, I may just refuel my retrorockets for Mars. Anyhow, the Peabody's in *Cambridge.*'

Liz shoved Danny back down on his pillow. 'Okay, Cambridge! Are you coming or not, damn it?'

'Holly who?'

'All right, smart-ass! Holly and I'll go alone, and you'll miss your chance to see a real extrasensory phenomena.'

'Phenomenon, singular,' Danny muttered, as he buried his head in the pillow.

But when Liz stormed out of the room, Danny was curious

enough to stumble out of bed over to the window. He got there in time to glimpse Liz and Holly skipping down the driveway. In the early morning light he could barely make out the two figures—Liz and a shorter girl with reddish hair who was dressed in a peculiar, old-fashioned patchwork dress and shawl. As he watched, the girls appeared to whisper to each other for a few seconds, then they sprinted full speed down the driveway through the snow toward the town road. 'Maybe I'll understand all of this when I wake up,' Danny mumbled to himself as he made his way back to bed. 'Was that Holly or Molly?'

'You need boots,' Liz said. 'Are you warm enough?'

'My shoes are sturdy and my shawl warm. It is a fine morning. 'Snowy winter, a plentiful harvest,' Poor Richard said.'

'Who?'

'*Poor Richard's Almanack,* which my father used to read to me,' Holly said, casting a disappointed glance about. 'Why, I even recognize the old church steeple over there. For years I have been hearing about the wonders of the modern era, but things here look just as I remember them. Where is your progress?'

Liz realized that Holly did not understand that nearby Old Sturbridge Village was a model colonial village, a careful recreation of how people lived in the eighteenth century. Of course it didn't surprise Holly! Just as Liz was about to launch into a lecture on the differences between Sturbridge and a place like New York City, a Corvette Stingray rounded the curve in the road ahead of them and whizzed by at top speed. Holly shrieked at the top of her lungs and ran behind a tree.

'You see, Holly, some things *are* different. That is known as an automobile. It's lots faster than horseback riding.'

Holly recovered her composure. 'For a minute there I thought we were witnessing a visitation of Ezekiel's fiery four-wheeled chariot. You know what the Bible says: "It was bronze below, shining crystal above, and a sound like the thunder of the Almighty."'

The car headed toward them now was certainly no 'fiery chariot' but a rickety old Model A driven by an elderly lady in a wide-brimmed hat whom Liz's Sturbridge friends had told her about. She was Mrs Beecher, the town's librarian and prize eccentric. 'Beggars can't be choosers,' Liz said, sticking out her thumb. The ancient car ground to a halt with a wrenching squeal.

Liz hopped in and Holly reluctantly followed. What made this vehicle go? Was it driven without any reins? But she would trust Liz. After all, this was Liz's century they were in now. Mrs Beecher began to lecture them on the evils of their ways. 'It isn't really safe for two young girls to be out hitchhiking like this,' she remonstrated as she swerved back into her own lane, missing an oncoming milk truck by inches.

'That's so far out...I mean yes, ma'am,' spluttered Liz, sneaking a terrified glance at Holly who didn't know that Mrs Beecher's driving was in any way unusual and so was beginning to relax and enjoy the experience.

'We are journey-bound to Boston and Cambridge town, Holly added, rewarding Mrs Beecher with her most charming smile.

'My, my. What a pleasure to hear such excellent diction. Of course, hitchhiking can be risky for the driver as well. You can't be too careful whom you pick up. Now, for example, I almost passed by you tow young ladies, because of the way one of you is dressed.'

'Holly,' whispered Liz. 'Maybe we had better get you some *real* clothes when we get to Cambridge.'

'In a recent survey of arrested murderers, robbers, and auto thieves,' Mrs Beecher went on, 'nearly all of the criminals were wearing blue denim jeans at the time of their capture. So you see, dear,' she said turning to Liz, 'wearing those trousers nearly lost you this ride. Why can't you wear something nice and ladylike like the outfit your little friend here has on.'

Liz kept quiet for the rest of the trip, not even daring to object when Mrs Beecher found them another 'safe' ride for the last leg of their journey, this time in the back of a national guard troop carrier truck. When they neared the city limits, the guardsmen, who regarded the presence of two stowaways as a great practical joke on their commanding officer, told the girls to hide under a pile of blankets. Thus Holly saw nothing of the modern city until the truck deposited them in Cambridge on the south side of Massachusetts Avenue.

*B*ehind the girls rose the enormous raw concrete bulk of the University Health Services building. Holly stared at it. It was the biggest building she had ever seen. 'What manner of person lives in that?' she asked.

'People work there. They don't live there,' Liz said and began to realize how much explaining she would soon have to do.

Holly's eyes were darting every which way, trying to take in the whole scene in one fell swoop. Cambridge was at its liveliest. Student wives in jogging suits strode on the snowy pavements carrying babies on their backs like papooses; tweedy, bearded scholars walked purposefully, puffing their pipes; booted suburban matrons who had driven into Cambridge to shop trudged along carrying kitchen utensils and leather goods; a nearsighted professor precariously balancing a huge stack of books slid on an icy patch. Liz made her way carefully across two heavily trafficked streets, while Holly followed her, oblivious to any danger from the cars: At the kiosk in the centre of Harvard Square, Liz bought a black and white map of the university from a toothless old newspaper vendor. As Liz studied the map with ferocious concentration, Holly's bright eyes drank everything in. When she saw a man in a turban followed by a woman in a bright red sari, she said, 'Have bands of Saracens and Canaanites pitched their tents nearby? Is it always so busy here?'

Liz was so preoccupied she barely heard Holly. 'Who are you talking about?' she answered. 'There aren't nearly as many students here as usual. I guess most left for vacation.'

Suddenly a Frisbee floated past Holly's nose. Liz caught the Frisbee midair and sent it soaring back.

'Shall we leave here...with no time wasted?' Holly said quickly, edging closer to Liz.

They walked along outside the wall of the campus, toward a gate which led into Harvard Yard. The stately red brick buildings began to fill Holly with a sense of calm. The clean snow covering the lawn, the greyish sky, the leafless trees were natural to her and made her feel a kind of serenity and belonging, as if things had not really changed so much after all.

Holly and Liz stopped to get their bearings. Standing before the austere grey stone of University Hall, they stared up at the statue of solemn, patriarchal John Harvard, who stared back down at them benignly. He was wearing knee socks and breeches and clasped a Bible.

'I rather like him,' said Holly. 'He's handsome, indeed.'

'He's older than you by more than a hundred years,' Liz teased. 'Definitely too old for you, even if he looks young for his age. Dad always used to say that nothing in Harvard Yard has changed for hundreds of years, since it was all so perfect from the start.'

'Your father knew the value of the things of the past. The finest schools are the old schools, the finest books are the old books, and the...'

'What about old food?' said Liz, trying to catch Holly off guard.

Holly was not put off. She answered softly, 'The finest wine is vintage wine. The finest cheese is aged cheese.'

As though she had just said something very weighty, Holly

59

whirled with a kind of bravado and bent to pick up a handful of snow which she threw at Liz. The unpacked flakes fluttered to the ground.

'Smart one,' Liz said, as she packed a tight snowball. 'Let me educate you in the fine art of the snowball.'

The two girls, laughing now, rounded the corner onto Divinity Street and walked down the pavement past an empty parking lot. Liz realized Holly was wise beyond her years, although she had the innocence of a child. The brisk air turned Holly's lips a beautiful scarlet.

'There,' said Liz, pointing to the large brick building. 'That's the museum, just like in the book. We're here.'

'There seems to be no one in attendance, though,' Holly said. Together they went up the stone stairs. Taped on the glass inside the entrance door was the small sign: MUSEUM CLOSED DURING THANKSGIVING RECESS.

Tears welled up in Liz's eyes. 'What can we do, Holly? We can't have come all this way for nothing. Maybe Danny was right.'

'Do not give up yet, Liz. Perchance we can find a residence in which to stay until the museum opens again.'

While Liz was wondering where that would be, a stooped, prematurely balding young man made his way up the stairs past them, then turned back to them. 'I'm sorry. The museum is closed today,' he said. 'Usually people don't look quite so disappointed as you two do.'

'We wanted to see the Maya Indian things,' Liz explained. 'You see, my father is an archaeologist who lectures here occasionally, and we have a pendant we want to compare to one of the stones in your collection. He's lost, and ...'

'Wait a minute. You wouldn't be Melville Dutton's daughter by any chance, would you?'

Liz nodded.

'Well, isn't that something,' the man said. 'I'm Jeff Fulton. I'm a graduate student here in mesoamerican anthropology. I know all about your father's work. Here, come on in with me. I work here, even on holidays, and the guard can let us in.' Jeff Fulton pressed the small white button beside the door.

60

Together they entered the dark museum. The guard, chiding Jeff about working too hard, opened the door to the director's outer office. They entered. 'We have to go downstairs,' said Jeff. 'That's where my office is.'

Jeff led the way to the stairway. Below they turned and passed through a maze of narrow hallways and rooms and entered the dark basement.

'This way, past the lounge,' Jeff directed them. They walked slowly on the concrete floor down a narrow hallway enclosed by storage shelves and drawers. On the left were offices. Jeff paused at one of the doors. Its glass panel was covered with wire mesh.

'It doesn't look like much, does it?' he said, smiling and turning a key in the lock. 'But some pretty great archaeologists have done their research behind these doors. They're my inspiration.' They entered and Jeff flicked a light switch. The fluorescent bulbs hummed, then bathed the room in bright white light. 'My desk,' Jeff said. 'There in the corner. Here, I'll get you some chairs.'

When they were seated, he said, 'I have to tell you, the exhibit isn't here. Right now it's at the American Museum of Natural History in New York, but it won't be there too long, I think. In fact tomorrow may be the last day. It goes on to Los Angeles on Monday.'

'Liz,' Holly said suddenly. 'Show Master Fulton that pendant you are wearing. Perchance he can tell us something about it.'

Jeff looked at Holly to see whether she was teasing with her archaic English. What was her costume all about, anyway? But he forgot about Holly when he looked at the jade Liz handed him.

'That's really beautiful,' he said, 'and it looks like an important piece to me. I don't know that much about the hieroglyphic writing—it's not my specialty—but one of these tiny glyphs on the back may be what is called an emblem glyph, probably the name of an ancient Maya city,' Jeffrey said. 'I've seen it somewhere before. And just recently...I know! It's on one of the casts that the Guatemalan government

61

sent us! The Tikal stela. That's in the New York exhibit right now.'

'A stela. Does that have something to do with the stars?' Holly asked, perplexed.

'No, no. Stelae are big stone monuments. The Maya set them up to commemorate special dates and events. You see, the Maya were obsessed with time. They had calendars inside of calendars on top of calendars. This jaguar may represent a very special dynasty of rulers and their city. I'm not sure, though. There are so many different kinds of jaguars in Maya art. Your father was very interested in this sort of thing, Liz. He thought the stelae might contain mathematical messages—formula—even more sophisticated than those we give them credit for. He was particularly interested in their astronomy. Of course, things like this pendant and the monuments have immense value as art objects, too, and that's part of the problem.'

'What problem?' Liz asked.

'Well, it's really hard for scholars to keep up with the art thieves. Things are looted and sold every day. The result is that scholars often can't prove their theories about what the Maya were writing about, because the writing has been disappearing into private collections.'

'Is it that the pendant is part of a formula, then, or a calculation?' Holly asked.

'It could be. It would be interesting to see if the Tikal stela text ties into it. If I can help,' Jeffrey said to Liz, 'let me know.'

'Thanks,' Liz said warmly. 'We need all the friends we can get on this one.'

Jeff Fulton led the girls back through the labyrinth of the darkened museum and outside again. 'If I could, I'd show you some of the things in the storeroom, but it's better if you come back when the museum is open. Or the library. I forgot to tell you there's a lovely wall panel over in the Tozzer Library, with glyphs all over it. Come back just for that, if you can. It's well worth it.'

'Thanks again, Jeff.' Liz and Jeff shook hands, and the student disappeared into the museum again.

'The pendant is part of a code,' Holly said. 'We must get to the New York exhibit. What mode of travel shall we employ?'

Liz immediately began rummaging in her backpack and pulled out two dog-eared bus tickets. 'I have an easy way.' Holly's presence gave Liz confidence and a secure feeling.

In a supper club in the near North Side of Chicago Elaine Dutton was nursing her after-dinner brandy and trying to remember how a woman acts on a date. She wondered how to relax without feeling guilty. Cigarette smoke was thick all around her. The scene was clearly singles, and the women were *Vogue* billboards—twenties to thirty-five. The men laughed hollowly over the sound of swirling ice cubes. As couples around them began heading for the crowded dance floor, Elaine studied her companion, Hal Abbot. He clearly had something more personal to discuss with his boss than the spring list at their publishing house.

Hal was in his mid-forties and had been an editor at Reynolds Publishing for five years. His personal interest, long before it became fashionable, was jogging and general physical fitness. He was a man who took pride in organizing every facet of his life with precision, which made him lonely in an imprecise world. Now there's a man who would never lose himself in a jungle, Elaine told herself as she sat warming her brandy snifter. And no doubt I'm the only woman who considers this a disqualifying defect.

When Mel was alive—when he was known to be alive—there were times when she had found Hal's interest in her flattering. Tonight, when she had every right to be seriously interested, she was distracted by Hal's tan. He hadn't been anywhere near the south for months, she thought. He must use a sunlamp. The thought of Mel Dutton under a sunlamp suddenly made her smile, and Hal, taking it as a sign of encouragement, warmed to the subject he had been trying delicately to lead to. 'About the kids, Elaine. You've done a great job with them. You really have. A heroic job. For kids without a father, they're absolutely...'

'They have a father, Hal.'

10/8   1183   63

'You know what I mean. You've got to face reality.'

'All right, Hal. Let's just say I'm really not in the mood to discuss it. How about a dance?'

'I'm sorry, Elaine, I haven't had a chance to study up on disco yet. Wouldn't want to make a fool out of myself.'

'Of course, Hal. I wouldn't want you to either. Let's talk about next year's books for a minute. I think the occult is going to be out soon. Maybe it's the right time for some adventure writers...'

Elaine's mind drifted back to her first meeting with her husband at the Explorer's Club. A group of renowned anthropologists and archaeologists had gathered for one of his lectures. He was absolutely charming and charismatic. His enthusiasm and his sense of humour made him a first-class press agent for anthropology and archaeology. She couldn't wait to meet him for the interview, although she felt a little inadequate for the occasion.

When later in the evening they were actually alone together in the deserted lobby of the club, they talked about his days at Harvard and about the books he had read as a child. They were from different worlds, but both of them soon knew it didn't make any difference. They created a certain kind of energy together, something that was beyond either one of them as individuals...

She turned back to Hal. 'I'm sorry, I didn't hear what you said.'

*A*gatha Dutton began putting away the groceries John had just brought from Sturbridge market. That is, she was trying to.

John had met Mrs Beecher, and that always led to an irresistible impulse to give his wife a performance. Although dressed in denim overalls, his every gesture, his voice and his face *were* Edna Beecher.

'I tell you, John Dutton,' he mimicked in a frosty voice, 'I don't know what Sturbridge is coming to. A hippie hitchhiker. And so young, too. Just about twelve, I'd say.' He minced around, talking directly into Agatha's face.

She backed away, giggling at his impersonation. 'Honestly, John Dutton, you are too much. Her idea of a hippie is probably anyone in jeans.' With that, she looked down at her own faded blue jeans and laughed again.

'The other,' continued John, enjoying his role, 'was dressed quite normally in a charming calico patchwork dress.' The word 'charming' was spread out over three syllables.

Both John and Agatha had found it a strain to follow their daughter-in-law's instruction not to discuss Mel's disappearance in front of Liz. John, with his New England sense of values, believed that Elaine was misguided in not letting her daughter confront the reality of her father's death, while Agatha clung to the notion that Mel might still be alive. Maybe it was next to impossible for anyone not a Maya to exist alone, lost in that jungle for so many months, but Mel Dutton was not just any archaeologist. Agatha, like Liz, held on to her hope.

Yesterday, with Liz and Danny present, had been the first time in weeks that they hadn't argued about the subject. So Danny's news this morning that Liz had gone off to play for the day with one of her local friends made them feel that at least they had put on a good show in front of the children.

But now, trying to make sense of Edna Beecher's latest delusion, Agatha brought John about abruptly. 'You're not suggesting it was Liz hitchhiking to Boston?' she demanded. There was something about patchwork that rang a bell. But it couldn't be...Danny had told them Liz had gone out to play with someone from over in Old Sturbridge.

Just then the door slammed, and Danny entered the kitchen, shedding ski poles, gloves, and other paraphernalia with every step. Melissa bounded from the living room to greet him and then ran off with one of the gloves. She held it gently in her mouth and waited for him to come after it.

'Hey, son, how was the downhill skiing?' asked John. 'As good as our cross-country yesterday?'

'Neat! But the bus coming back stalled with about forty people on board, and I had to help the driver get her started. The motor was flooded. Is Liz back?'

'No, I guess she and her Sturbridge friend are having a good time,' Agatha said cheerily. 'What did you say her name was?'

'Holly. Holly Patches.'

'Patches?' John said, startled. 'You mean her last name is *Patches?*'

'Nah. I just call her patches 'cause that's what she wears. She's supposed to be an *ancestor.*'

Just then the telephone rang. Danny, who had stuffed a handful of gingersnaps into his mouth, raced into the hall to answer it while John and Agatha looked at each other in disbelief.

'Hello?...Oh, you...Boston, huh. Why should I...I came up here to ski and the skiing's great...gingersnaps...no, it's

66

not disgusting. Chewing is a normal physiological function, just like...Okay, okay. Run that by me again...so you're going to New York tonight. I suppose you want us to call Mum and make up some story about why you're coming home early. Listen, Liz, if your friend is really from the past, she can slip us the American History answers for our exams...No, it's all right. I'll con Grandma into doing it...'Bye.'

'That was Liz, wasn't it?' said Agatha from the doorway.

'Yeah, she and that other girl are taking the bus to New York. They want you to call Mum and warn her.'

'Bus? New York? Well, so she *was* Edna's hitchhiker. Bad business, that...' Agatha said slowly. 'But I suppose Liz would rather be safe at home when she's grieving. I told Elaine that when she had this idea of shipping Liz up here for the long weekend. At least your mother is home from Chicago by now. She was supposed to get in sometime today. I just wish we knew who the other girl's folks were so we could call them and make sure they know where she is.'

'Agatha, dear, I have a feeling that won't be necessary.' John smiled sagely, as Danny, for once in his life thrown off balance by an adult, wondered what Grandpa might know about Liz's friend in patchwork.

Liz emerged from the phone booth in the small waiting room of the Greyhound Bus Terminal. She moved past rows of dingy metal lockers, rest rooms, a few benches, and a coffee vending machine. Liz looked quizzically at her friend who was now seated, her carpetbag beside her. 'I just talked to Danny. He's going to help us...but Holly, he wanted to know if you perform miracles...Do you?'

'No, unfortunately, I am merely human. It seems to me that it is you and Daniel who have a miraculous capacity. Did he truly hear you from such a distance?' Shaking her head, Holly murmured, 'I suppose he must have...'

And Liz wondered how to explain Alexander Graham Bell's invention to Holly.

'*Attention!* All passengers for New York, report to gate three immediately. We are scheduled to leave at eighteen hundred hours. That is in one minute, naught seven seconds; I repeat . . . '

'I wish you hadn't called him "Captain," ' Liz whispered crossly to her seatmate. 'We're trying to be inconspicuous, remember? Now you've got him going on this silly game pretending he's on a ship instead of a bus.'

'I verily wish we were on an airplane,' said Holly unabashed. 'I have never seen one and so must accept your word that machines can fly. You twentieth-century folk! I cannot imagine why you do not savour life as people did in my day.'

As it happened, Holly had been savouring life so much that Liz was exhausted trying to keep up with her and her questions. She drifted off into a half sleep, only to be startled sometime later by another self-important announcement from the driver.

'For the safety of the passengers, remember, no smoking cigarettes, no lighting matches, and please maintain good posture at all times.'

'What's going on . . . where are we?' Liz muttered, shaking her head to clear the cobwebs.

'We are here in the twentieth century,' Holly replied, sitting up straight in compliance with the driver's last directive.

Distracted by some odd noises across the aisle, Liz glanced sideways. What she saw made her face turn bright red and she quickly sneaked a look at Holly, wondering whether she, too, had noticed what the couple over there was doing. Holly was staring at the scene with great interest.

'Is that what you used to call bundling?' Liz ventured.

'Oh, no,' Holly objected. 'The rule in bundling was that the boy and girl must have a board between. These people here are having conversation . . . and love. Or perhaps merely something physical without love.' she added helpfully.

Stunned, Liz gulped and regarded her old-fashioned friend. 'How much do you know, Holly?'

'Only what I ought.' Holly sniffed. 'A girl is not ready for courting and marriage until she is fifteen.'

'My mother didn't get married until she was twenty-eight,' Liz said.

Holly's face took on a pained look. 'I am sorry. Was there a family tragedy to cause such a delay?'

68

Liz did not answer, but she was beginning to wonder if she could ever get the upper hand with Holly. At least she was sure that Holly's first view of the Manhattan skyline at night would impress her.

And, she was right! From the moment the New York skyline came into sight, Holly gasped with amazement. She couldn't come up with any comparisons from the Bible or anywhere else. 'How verily beautiful,' she said, lost in the fairyland of lights and shapes.

Midnight. Night people—panhandlers, hustlers, pushers, streetwalkers—had crowded into the New York Port Authority Bus Terminal because of the cold, plying their trade with the commuters and tourists. Liz urged Holly to walk quickly to avoid any undesirable confrontations.

Holly was mystified at first by the moving steps of the escalator, but by the time she reached the bottom, she was addicted. She made a round trip up and down before Liz could whisk her into a taxi.

As soon as they climbed in the cab, the driver inquired in a Brooklyn accent, 'Where to, ladies?' Then he popped in a tape cassette. Suddenly Holly and Liz were being treated to Bach's Brandenburg Concerto # 5.

'Seventy-ninth and Park,' said Liz.

In a lull between the concerto's movements, they could hear the driver grumbling to himself, 'Terrific. Seventy-ninth and Park. The whole city's fulla dough. . . I pick up two little girls. With that get up one of 'em had on, I thought she was some rich old dame. Another lousy tip. I oughta have my peepers examined.'

When they were almost there, he turned around and quickly eyed Holly up and down. He gave her a big bearish grin and said, 'You goin' to a masquerade?'

Only Liz laughed. And they continued their midnight ride to the Dutton apartment.

The gaudy neon signs lit up Holly's face and turned it all colours as she stared, openmouthed, at the people and the general confusion of the night streets.

The taxi passed McDonald's. Looking out at redheaded

Ronald McDonald, smiling benignly and holding a hamburger, Holly recalled the image of benevolent John Harvard. 'What university did he found?'

'That's MacDonald's, the biggest hamburger institution in the world.'

They strode through the apartment lobby toward the wood-panelled elevator. Liz couldn't help feeling some satisfaction at the thought that the ride to the twenty-second floor might just satisfy Holly's desire to fly.

Holly did not make so much as a whimper of complaint, but by the time they reached the door to the apartment, she looked a little shaky. Liz hastily opened the door, sat Holly down on the big couch—where Holly glanced with confusion at the modern furnishings so unlike those at Sturbridge—and went to look for her mother. There was no answer to her 'Hello...Mum?' and Liz returned to the living room where Holly, now quite recovered, was staring at a white envelope bearing Liz's name that lay in the centre of the coffee table. Liz snatched up the envelope and ripped it open.

'What luck,' she cried. 'Mum has gone to Washington to see an author. Grandma's phone call came just as she was about to leave for the airport. She left me some money and a couple of credit cars with a letter of authorization. She'll be back on Monday.'

Relieved that she wouldn't have to try to explain Holly's existence to her mother, Liz decided to show off the apartment to Holly. As she expected, Holly was delighted by the kitchen sink, the dishwasher, and the automatic washer-dryer. She was doubtful, however, about the bathroom—no matter how many times Liz explained modern plumbing, Holly still felt there was something not quite clean about having an outhouse *in* the house. Liz finally gave up on this point and ushered Holly back to the kitchen where she pulled a large steak from the freezer and popped it into the microwave oven. Holly, meanwhile, became engrossed in examining the pantry supply of goods, pulling the cans one by one from the birchwood cabinet and exclaiming over the labels.

'Did your mother paint all of these?' she asked reverently,

staring at a can which pictured a ripe Italian plum tomato. 'It is an admirable likeness, and she has copied the pattern correctly every time.'

'Of course she didn't paint them. Anyway, can labels aren't art!' Liz suddenly remembered the old Andy Warhol poster of a Campbell's soup can that used to hang in the hall near Danny's bedroom.

'Look, Holly,' she said, dragging her by the hand into the living room and pointing out a framed print of Picasso's *Woman in Blue.* 'That's modern art.'

Holly looked doubtful. 'But that is not a good likeness at all.'

Desperate, Liz indicated a huge macramé wall hanging.

Holly giggled. 'Looks like a horse chewed it.' Then her eyes fell on a piece of brightly patterned cloth that hung on the far wall. 'That is much better,' she said as if trying to make amends. 'It took a practiced hand with a loom to create that.'

'That's a handwoven serape—a kind of shawl—from the Lake Atitlán region in Guatemala. Every young girl invents her own private variation in the design. That serape is almost one hundred years old, I believe.'

'Did I not say that the old things are the best?'

'Just you wait,' Liz muttered under her breath as she went to retrieve their steak. The microwave oven had switched off automatically; the steak was medium rare and juicy. Liz noticed that Holly's suspicion of the properties of the magical oven did not prevent her from eating her share.

By the time they finished eating, Liz was so tired that she could hardly hold her head up. There were so many questions that she wanted to ask Holly, so much she didn't understand about her new friend. But Holly, who did not seem eager to talk, wandered off to the bathroom where she discovered the shower and was soon splashing contentedly. Liz headed for her room and pulled back the spread on both beds. She was in her own bed and half asleep when she heard Holly emerging from the bathroom, humming a familiar melody.

Funny, Liz thought as she lost consciousness...doesn't sound like colonial music at all. I recognize that ballad from somewhere.... *'Yesterday, all my troubles...'*

71

*T*he next morning Liz rummaged in her closet and held a plaid skirt and pea coat out to Holly. 'Would you like to borrow these? Your dress calls an awful lot of attention to us. And we're almost the same size.

'My thanks for your offer, but I believe I can shorten my dress to your fashion, if you will lend me a needle and thread. Oh, and shears, too,' said Holly, examining her costume in the mirror. 'But I do fancy the jacket...'

Her attention was caught by the bottles on Liz's dresser. 'All these creams and lotions. What are they for?' she asked.

'They're super. They're all advertised on TV.

'TV?' Holly asked.'

And Liz grew silent. How would she explain that electronic marvel?

'I simply wash my face and shade it from the sun with my bonnet,' Holly said. Liz looked enviously at Holly's clear complexion.

'What is this?' Holly picked up a tiny bottle of Charlie cologne. 'How lovely. May I?' Holly dabbed it knowingly

72

behind her ears and on her wrists. Liz realized how little need
there was for Holly to use the perfume, for Holly herself was
the scent of springtime blossoms. Liz looked at the smooth,
delicate hands holding the cologne and admired Holly's grace.

I guess that's the difference between us, Liz thought sadly.
She's really a lady like Mum wants me to be, and I'm just a . . .

The American Museum of Natural History was across
Central Park from the Dutton apartment. The morning was
icy. The two girls ran down a closed-off side street outside the
building. The next thing they knew, skateboards were
thundering all around them. Liz spotted her neighbour, Jimmy
Simpson, who seemed to be leading a group of boys in
acrobatic feats.

'Take it, Liz' he said, coming over.

Liz took the board and proceeded to show her stuff. She
whirled and twirled, and for the first time felt really proud in
front of Holly.

Jimmy turned to the stranger. 'Can you do that?' he asked
her.

Holly hesitated. 'It looks rather perilous,' she said.

'Come on, take a crack at it.'

Liz helped Holly climb on the board, and Jimmy put a hand
on Holly's waist to steady her. Then they both let go of her,
and she started to roll down the gentle incline, tottering a little.
A blush came onto Holly's cheeks as she lost her usual
confidence.

'Bend your knees more!' called Liz. 'You're too stiff!'

'Relax!' yelled Jimmy.

'You're doing terrific!' Liz called again.

Holly tried to lean forward in a sort of racing position, the
way she'd just watched Liz and the boys do it. The board shot
forward smack into a group of men coming out of a storefront
synagogue. They were wearing wide-brimmed black hats,
black skirted coats, and beards. One of the men bent down and
helped Holly off the ground. Another handed the board back to
her with a slight reprimand: 'You lost this, my child?'

Holly curtsied to the men, saying, 'I thank thee for thy

kindness. May goodness be with thee always.'

When the men started to head off, talking animatedly in Yiddish, Holly turned to Liz and said confidentially, 'The Quakers are a wonderful people.'

'Those are a religious sect of the Chasidic Jews!'

They walked through Central Park heading west. An occasional tiny snowflake fluttered down from the leaden sky to the ground, now asleep between colourful fall and flowering spring. 'Woods, trees, and rocks,' Holly said. 'We seem to be in the country again.'

'Just you wait,' Liz replied. 'You haven't seen anything yet.' Soon they emerged from the park directly across from the museum.

'That,' said Holly in awe, 'is truly the biggest building in the world. Even larger than the one in Cambridge town.'

'Wait'll you see the rest of Manhattan. It was too dark last night for you to see anything but the skyline. I'll get you close enough to show you how tall our buildings really are.'

'Very well, lead on.'

They crossed Central Park West.

All of her life Liz had felt hurried, as if she had been born late and had to catch up. Now, even though the museum was just opening, she sped up the steps, and Holly half tripped trying to keep up with her. When she spotted the statue of Teddy Roosevelt, Holly called out, 'Did he found a hamburger institution, too?'

Liz hurried her inside the cavernous foyer and up to the information desk.

'Yes?' inquired the woman behind the desk. 'May I help you?'

'We're looking for the exhibit about the Maya,' Liz said breathlessly.

'Oh, yes. The 'Children of the Sun' exhibition. Go down the hall—past the stuffed elephants, through the Akeley Gallery and the African Hall, and you'll be there.'

Liz and Holly turned the corner into the mesoamerican gallery and found themselves standing face to face with a ferocious

74

life-sized figure sporting an inmense feathered headdress. His half-open mouth revealed carefully filed front incisors inlaid with tiny circlets of jade. Startled as she was by the model's lifelike appearance, Liz couldn't help thinking there was something peculiar about its glassy stare. Then she realized...the man was cross-eyed!

At the entrance to the exhibit was a sign offering a recorded tour of the pieces on exhibit. Liz had enough money to rent the equipment for both.

The girls lined up with the other visitors as the museum attendant passed out portable tape cassette machines. The attendant helped them fit their respective earpieces.

'What in heaven's name is this?' asked Holly.

'This machine will tell us what all these things are.'

The attendant instructed, 'Push the switch to the "on" position.'

Holly did, then jumped as a well-modulated voice suddenly spoke into her ear:

> Hello. I'm Marshall Thompson, assistant curator of the American Museum of Natural History, and I would like to guide you through the 'Treasures of the Maya—Children of the Sun' exhibition, certainly one of the most dazzling of our times. You will see fifty beautiful pieces that have been found during the last century in various parts of the Maya area. Many are on loan for this momentous occasion from the governments of Mexico and Guatemala, and, before now, have never been seen outside those countries.
>
> Since I will not, unfortunately, have time to speak about every object with the detail it deserves, I encourage you to use the 'off' switch on your machine as often as you wish in order to study objects you find particularly fascinating. From time to time you will hear a sound like this...*beep*...that's the signal to

75

turn off your machine until you have reached the next object on the tour.

We will begin our exhibit with a reconstruction of an ancient Maya priest in full ceremonial regalia. This is how he might have appeared in the time between, say, A. D. 600 and 900. Notice the filed teeth first. This was done for many of the Maya elite. The T-shape that results from the filing is, in other contexts, a wind symbol. It's also one of the hallmarks of Kinich-Ahau, the sun god, as are the crossed eyes.

Make particular note of the clothing. The gigantic headdress is in the form of the head of a dragonlike creature. We've never found an actual headdress, but they are shown on some of the carvings you will see later. Probably they were of wickerwork or *papier-mâché*—something light, certainly, or they would have never stayed on.

Some of the crowd responded with smiles. The tape continued.

The feathers used by the Maya priests or rulers were those of the quetzal bird. These were borrowed from our ornithological collections, for the quetzal is now almost extinct. Not so in the seventh century, though. Their green colour must have made them particularly significant to the Maya, because green related to jade, to corn, to water—all things precious to the Maya.

'That means your green pendant is precious,' Holly said. Liz shushed her in order to listen to the recording.

Note the jaguar skins used in the trousers of the

figure. To the Maya of this period the jaguar—the most powerful and feared of the jungle animals—symbolized many things, among them, royalty. The jaguar also symbolized the sun in its night journey through the underworld. As you can see, Maya religion was very, very complicated.

In the display case beyond the partition in the next area, you will see some objects related to the origin of the Maya, marked below the red audio insignia guide as Exhibit Number Two. *Beep*.

Holly and Liz turned off their machines and walked toward the display. Holly was proud of herself for having mastered her push-button control so quickly. She was getting used to the twentieth century!

These figurines and large head were carved by a people we call the Olmecs. They built ceremonial centres and carved massive monuments between 1500 and 400 B. C. —*before* the Maya appeared on the scene. They also revered the jaguar, or more accurately the were-jaguar. Carved from a single piece of blue-green jade, this sculpture still retains the incredible polish that suggests it was a ritual piece. It is believed to be a model of a much larger one hidden in the Yucatán.

Holly Hobbie pulled on Liz's sleeve, but Liz shook her off.

This masterly creation is half-human, half-feline. Of even greater import is its significance in the Olmec and Maya religions. Indeed, these people worked jade as easily as if it were soft clay. We will go next to Exhibit Ten. *Beep*.

Liz and Holly pressed the buttons to stop their machines.

Liz peered through the glass of the display case at the small exquisitely carved stone. This was a jaguar all right, but one with human eyes and nose and a drooping, almost sinister, snarling mouth with large fangs—definitely not the same as the one on *her* pendant. 'There are so many jaguars, Holly. How will we ever find what mine means?'

'This voice in our ears may tell us yet if we let it.' They followed the rest of the group to a table model replica of Tikal.

The voice intoned:

> This is an extraordinary scale model of one of the places where Maya civilization began—the great city of Tikal, in what is now northern Guatemala. As early as 600 B. C. there was a settlement here, but it was not until the early years of the Christian era that the city began to grow to the proportions you see in this reconstruction. Here you see the city as it was around A. D. 850. Notice the towering pyramid platforms. The largest were a memorial to the dead and revered rulers. One, Temple IV, towers two hundred twelve feet above the level on which it was built—the tallest known Maya building. Great causeways connected the various temple roofs and the great plazas where ceremonial processions took place over the centuries. At its height, when Tikal looked like this, the city probably had a population of around fifty thousand. For reasons we do not yet fully understand, Tikal was abandoned, beginning about A. D. 900, and the surrounding jungle slowly reclaimed it. There are many unanswered questions about the Maya. The biggest mystery of all is why were places like Tikal suddenly abandoned?
>
> On the right wall of the second gallery is Exhibit Forty-one. *Beep.*

As they followed the crowd to the second gallery, Liz complained, 'This is as hard as my history class. And I'm flunking that. What good is this doing us, anyway?'

Holly answered, 'I cannot promise you it will help find your father, but I think it may. As Poor Richard said, "It is easy to see, hard to foresee." '

Liz groaned. 'Please, Holly, come off it. I have enough on my mind without your Poor Richard.'

They turned their machines back on.

> This delicately carved tableau contains the calendar. The Maya began their extremely accurate parallel systems on a specific date that matches our own August 10, 3114 B. C. And they believed their history would end with the next great cycle of their calendar, a date that will fall in our year 2013.
>
> The red audio insignias above on your left clearly mark the rest rooms and the water fountain. Please avail yourself of these courtesies.

Holly considered this part of the instructions and dutifully proceeded to line up at the fountain before she realized she had mistaken the suggestin of the voice on tape as a specific command.

'Liz, I don't want to rest. Do you? . . . But the voice said to.'

Liz smiled. 'I guess we don't need a drink either.'

'Switch it on again,' Holly said.

> Michael Coe, the great Maya expert from Yale and a seasoned member of many excavations, has stressed that we would be wrong to regard the Maya as primitive thinkers guided by superstition and myth. Coe regards Maya history as a kind of maze. 'Everywhere we turn,' he has said, 'we find that the Maya have set puzzles for us to solve.'

79

'I'll say,' Liz said grimly.

> We must remember that everything the Maya
> thought, wrote, and built was perfectly logical
> in the context of their culture. Their ways only
> seem puzzling and enigmatic because we lack
> the key—the Rosetta stone, if you will—that
> will enable our scholars to read their minds.

'Oh, wow! I know about that,' Liz announced smugly. 'The
Rosetta stone was the clue that broke the code of ancient
Egyptian writing.'

Holly nodded in acknowledgement but whispered, 'Ssh, I'm
trying to concentrate.' Liz remained thrilled at the thought that
she had remembered her history.

Pausing in front of a seven-foot-high stela monument, the
girls listened intently.

> Modern linguists and epigraphers have made a
> start on the task of deciphering Maya glyphs.
> But they are just beginning, and even if they
> succeed, the great bulk of Maya writing—the
> bark paper codices or screenfold books, which
> were no doubt far more detailed than any texts
> the Maya ever carved on stone—were
> destroyed by Spanish priests shortly after the
> conquest.
>
> Most of the great archaeologists have
> dreamed of finding a cache of Maya codices
> from the classic period. Perhaps such a treasure
> lies waiting to be discovered in some
> abandoned cave or hidden tomb—perhaps at
> some city yet undiscovered. Even a single
> codex would be a great find.
>
> For now those who study the Maya must
> concentrate on deciphering those texts that
> have already been found. Much of the existing
> Maya writings seem to deal with astronomy

and the complex Maya calendar, or with rulers and their dates of reign. Those of you who would like to know more of Maya astronomy are invited to attend our current star show at the Hayden Planetarium, entitled 'Ancient Stargazers.' The shows begin promptly on the hour. this concludes our recorded tour. Please take time to enjoy the exhibits we have not described.

Liz drifted away from the group. Taking a seat on a bench near a case full of painted Maya pottery, she tried to make sense of the lecture. Was it possible that her father had shared this dream of finding a lost city filled with precious manuscripts? Was he looking for such a city when he disappeared?

Liz stared glumly at a large Maya vase in the case to her right. Painted on its side was a picture of a bronze-skinned old man in loincloth and fancy headdress who appeared to be leaning against a wall. In one hand he held a fat cigar. The idea of a cigar-smoking Maya was really weird. 'He looks just like my grandfather!' she said aloud.

'Liz, Liz,' Holly interrupted excitedly. 'Over there! It is the stone we came to see...the one in the book!'

There it stood on a specially made pedestal, a great flat slab that towered over the girls. Framed between the parallel sides and arching top, a gigantic figure of a man carved in low relief in the whitish stone glowered at the spectators. He was dressed just like the mannequin in the hallway outside. The space beside and above the feathered headdress was filled with orderly rows of glyphs.

'It's exactly the same kind of writing as on the pendant!' Liz cried, starting to pull the jade ornament from around her neck for a better look.

'Do not, please do not,' Holly begged. 'If the guard sees that, he will surely think you purloined it from the exhibit!'

'I what? Oh, you mean stole it. You're right. But we just *have* to find out what those things *say.*'

81

'Here,' Holly said, stooping. 'Here is a card that may tell us.'

'Cast of Stela 40, Tikal, Guatemala,' read the caption framed behind glass on the monument's pedestal. 'Date: 9.10.0.0.0 1 Ahau 8 Kayab in the Maya calendar, equal to January 25, A. D. 633. This stela depicts a priest or ruler, probably of Tikal, the place where it was erected, and commemorates some event that took place earlier. The badly eroded glyphs conceal the exact time interval, but the event relates to another city, symbolized by the emblem glyph in position D4.' A diagram on the card showed where the glyph was on the monument above.

'There it is—our old friend, the jaguar,' cried Liz, pointing to the glyph on the monument above them. 'That's what Dad's notes meant. The jaguar on the pendant is the name of a city! And the stuff on the back refers to that city!' But then she grew despondent again. 'How will we ever figure out what this business is all about? You heard the guide. People spend their entire lives trying to understand the Maya.'

'Nonsense,' Holly said with finality. 'I am from the past, and you understand me, do you not?'

'Yes, when you stay away from that old Poor Richard of yours.'

'I agree, we cannot rely solely on him. As he himself said, "The ancients tell us what is best; but we must learn of the moderns what is fittest." ' Holly smiled to show that she was teasing with still another quote.

'Incredible! What'd you do, memorize that whole almanac? Holly, what are we gonna do?'

'Why do we not go to see the star show. The heathens set great store by the stars.'

Liz said, 'Okay, I'm game. But let's go. As my dad said, "Lost time is never found again." Now you've got me doing it!'

*L*iz and Holly rushed to the planetarium, managing to settle in their seats just as the noon show was getting under way. As the lights went down, a brilliant pattern of simulated stars flashed onto the dome above them, and Holly gasped audibly. 'I wondered where all the stars were when we arrived last night,' she said, elbowing Liz.

Liz sighed, trying to concentrate on the bright arrow that was zooming in on a point near the horizon of the dome. If only Danny were here. As far as she was concerned, when you'd seen one star, you'd seen them all.

> . . . Venus was, to the Romans, the mysterious
> goddess of love and beauty.

'Even I know that,' Liz said.

> To the Greeks, she was Aphrodite . . .

'I know Aphrodite,' whispered Holly importantly, 'and I

know some Greek. *Aphro* means 'mist' or 'clouds,' and *dite* conveys the idea of shining...So Aphrodite's name means something like, "she who shines through the clouds." '

Liz, impressed, did a double take and looked at Holly with renewed respect.

> ...Venus is second only to the moon as the brightest natural object in Earth's night sky, completely covered with a cloud layer. It is the closest neighbour to Earth in space—that is, the planet whose orbit moves closest to Earth. As a matter of fact it appears that tiny Earth, rather than the massive sun, may be controlling the spin of Venus and conversely that Venus may exercise some mysterious influence over Earth. In any event the spin of Venus seems to be closely tied to the relative orbits of Earth. As Professor Anthony Aveni of Colgate University has said, Venus appears to be hitched to the sun by an imaginary elastic line upon which the planet bobs back and forth like a yo-yo...

When Liz looked over at Holly, the girl was staring at the starry display, as if to solve the mystery of Venus right there.

> We have so many questions about Venus. Recently NASA made the first penetration of this very strange and peculiar cloud layer when *Pioneer Venus I* was launched.
>
> Note the movement of the arrow. Venus is moving a few degrees to the north, rising before the sun. It has now reached its nothern-most point on the horizon. These movements of the stars and even the time of sunrise at different periods of the year are correlated with the stones of Stonehenge, the temples of the Maya, and perhaps even some circular rock patterns

in Wyoming, according to the findings of Professor Herschel Goodman of the University of Pennsylvania in the late 1960s. Recently, Professor Goodman, working with field anthropologists like the late Melville Dutton, further substantiated his theory that many of the monuments of the Maya and others were nothing more than markers that served as astral observatories. . .

Liz, hearing her father referred to as the 'late' Professor Dutton, squirmed and fought off tears. Before the show was over, she tugged at Holly and whispered hoarsely, 'I've got to get some air.'

As they left the auditorium, Holly lay a comforting hand on Liz's arm. 'It is all right,' she soothed. 'It means nothing. After all, I am the "late" Holly Hobbie, am I not?'

'You're right, Holly. I've got to keep from being emotional. That's what Mother keeps telling me, too. But I still don't understand what all this stuff is about. Do you?'

'No, but I think we have been given a sign.'

'A sign? I didn't get a sign. All I got was more confused.'

' "Tis a gift to be simple," ' Holly answered smiling. 'Is it possible for us to go to Pennsylvania and see Professor Herschel Goodman?'

'You mean let him figure out the message for us?'

'That is my meaning.'

'Wait a sec. First I'll call Danny. He may have some ideas. He's *very* scientific. Let's go home!'

Sprinting home, they arrived at the apartment lobby red-faced and breathless, and raced straight up for the phone. No answer. It went without saying, she thought. Danny wasn't sitting around waiting for her call in the middle of the day. Not when the fields and woods were full of clean, beautiful cross-country ski trails.

Liz threw herself into a deep armchair. 'Now what'll we do?'

Holly didn't say anything. She was sitting on the window seat gazing down on New York City. From her vantage point she could see past the bare tree branches sprawled against the barren backdrop of the park to where buses were crawling like a caravan of caterpillars.

Liz tried again to get Holly's attention, but Holly was mesmerized. Liz went over to the window. 'Look, a horse and buggy,' Holly said, her voice filled with nostalgia.

Liz decided that if she and Holly were going to accomplish anything, she'd have to give Holly a crash course on the ways of the modern world. Otherwise every new thing that came along would distract her. And, anyway, what else were they going to do while they waited until Danny returned to the farmhouse.

Beginning the tour with essentials, Liz said, 'Hungry, Holly? Let me buy you a hot dog.'

Holly had a bad case of culture shock until Liz explained that eating a 'hot dog' didn't mean what she probably thought. Holly was even persuaded to try one with sauerkraut. Then Liz took her nineteenth-century friend by the hand and pulled her down the steps into the subway. While Liz stopped at the token booth, Holly tried to straight-arm her way past the turnstile. 'What manner of gate is this that does not swing?' she asked. Before she could back up for another try, Liz deposited a token and led the surprised Holly through.

From the stairs the girls could see the train pulling into the Lexington Avenue station. They whizzed down to the platform as multicoloured graffiti and advertisements flashed by them on all sides. Liz pulled Holly through the crowd toward the rear window of the last car. Holly was still adjusting her sunbonnet as they watched the tunnel lights recede.

The noise of the subway and the passengers jostling against her frightened Holly, but she was determined not to show it. She asked Liz quietly, 'How long is this phase of our travels?' Liz assured her that they would soon change to an express train and then the trip would be faster. But Holly did not really breathe easily until they made their way back up into daylight at Fulton Street. Liz led her the few blocks to the World Trade Center and then watched her friend's reaction.

'What hath God wrought?' Holly exclaimed, looking up at

the 110-storey buildings. 'What hath *man* wrought?'

The elevator ride to the tower and their first steps out onto the observation deck made them both a little uneasy. The distinctions between Liz the tour guide and Holly the tourist began to disappear. As they looked down over a toy city with a miniature population, over New Jersey on one side, Staten Island, Brooklyn, The Bronx, and Queens and clear up to Connecticut on the other, both girls were overcome with reverent fascination.

Liz pointed out the piers, the back of historic Trinity Church with its graveyard, the edge of Chinatown, and the Soho artists' section. It was incredible to Holly. Buildings everywhere, cars everywhere, people everywhere...her mind struggled to absorb it all. There were more people in any one section than she had ever encountered in her lifetime.

When they were back on the ground, Holly asked, 'What is next?'

'Were gonna take a bus to Greenwich Village.'

'In England!' Holly exclaimed.

'No,' Liz laughed. 'This is New York's Greenwich Village. A lot of famous artists and writers used to live there—my mum did when she first came to New York. Mum says that all young people should start out here,' she finished.

They ogled the shop windows, admired the charming private houses with their cottage-style façades, and breathed deeply all the marvellous aromas.

Holly had never seen so many kinds of foods in her life. Greek, Italian, Lebanese, macrobiotic health foods, tea and spices from twenty different countries: every time she looked around, it was as though she were experiencing another part of the world. 'Have they crammed the entire planet into a few city blocks?' she asked. And when Liz led her to the thirty-one flavours of Baskin-Robbins, she was not only overwhelmed but also starved. First she had a question: 'Please, Liz, tell me truly, is a Rocky Road edible?'

Next Liz showed her the wonders of Fifth Avenue. The store windows with their abundance of alluring outfits, furs, and jewels made Holly's eyes grow wider. But so did the prices!

'My father used to take care of all our needs on a few pence a week!'

Later, standing at the edge of the fountain at Lincoln Center, Holly gazed up at the Chagall murals in the Metropolitan Opera building. 'All these houses of music, dance, and mime. There certainly should be no excuse in this city for an idle mind.' With a hint of apology in her voice, Holly concluded: 'I see you moderns have more than a reason or two for being proud.'

All Liz could do was beam.

As they entered the apartment, Liz kicked off her boots and stretched out on the couch. 'I'm pooped,' she said. Then, affecting Holly's manner, she added, 'Well, now that I've regaled you with the wonders of the modern world, shall we partake of a bit of respite?'

'Yes, indeed,' Holly agreed.

The telephone sounded its shrill ring before they had a chance to drop off.

'Hello....oh, Danny! I tried to call earlier but you were out! Listen, are you alone? Can you talk?'

Danny answered in a hushed voice, 'What's goin' on? What're you two crazies doing?'

Liz told him about their morning at the museum, jumbling it a little. When Danny tried to make her repeat, she didn't have the patience for it. 'Listen, are you going to help or just keep quizzing me, you creep?'

'Easy, sis. Just let me have the part about Professor Goodman again.'

'They said he worked with Dad on a lot of his theories.'

'Maybe,' Danny suggested, 'since it's only an hour and a half away, you ought to go see him. Of course, you won't know the right questions to ask, but...'

'Could you come? Please, Danny! We really need you!'

Danny was unusually gentle in his reply. He knew this was no time for kidding. 'I'd love to, Liz, but Grandma and Grandpa would be hurt if I left them too. Anyhow, you can always call me if you get stuck. Meanwhile, I can cover for you here—and with Mum.'

'Okay. 'I'll let you know what we find out. Thanks, Danny.'

Not wishing to appear sentimental to Liz, Danny concluded, 'Take care of yourself, knucklehead. Don't do the usual female dumb stuff. And just make sure you keep in touch.'

'Will do, Danny. First thing tomorrow, then,' she said, summoning up her resources, 'Holly and I go to Philly.'

Holly seemed ready to leave for Philadelphia the second Liz hung up. She was pacing back and forth with an excited look on her face. Suddenly, pausing with great solemnity, she clasped her hands and looked heavenward. 'With fervent supplication to the Almighty Being, that we may be safely delivered to the Seat of Independence.'

'Come down and rejoin us mortals,' Liz said.

Holly proclaimed, 'Philadelphia, I trust you know, is the birthplace of the United States. There, beneath the Liberty Bell, assembled the wisest men in all the nation, the Founding Fathers.'

'You mean Washington, Jefferson, Franklin, and all those people? None of them are around anymore.'

'Of course they are not. Except that Benjamin Franklin seems to be with us,' Holly said slyly.

'What do you mean?'

'Well, he is the Poor Richard I keep quoting to you. Richard Saunders was the name he made up for himself.'

'Enough. Let's talk about *now* for a change. Besides, I've got news for you, Holly. The Liberty Bell's cracked.'

Holly considered a moment. 'Incidentally, do we have the funds to reach Philadelphia?'

'Yeah, we have the funds—courtesy of Master Charge and American Express. Oh, Holly, do you think I should try to get in touch with Mother first? She might try to talk us out of things if I do.'

' "Honour thy father and thy mother," ' quoted Holly. 'That is the Fourth Commandment. On the other hand, in your situation, how can you possibly honour both?'

'You're right, Holly. We'll skip calling her. You know, you're not the only one who knows proverbs. I just thought of another: "Desperate times call for desperate measures." Let's put an album on and get some sleep.'

*T*he silver cars of the Metro-
liner glided into Philadelphia's Thirtieth Street Station at
precisely eleven-twenty.

'Not unlike the museum yesterday,' Holly noted, gazing at
the huge room of the main station—an ornate chamber of stone
that dwarfed all human activity within it and made the frantic
business of catching trains seem quite insignificant. 'What now?'

'I'll try to reach Dr Goodman at home,' answered Liz. 'It's
Sunday and I'm sure he'll be there. You wait here, by the coffee
machine.' Liz then disappeared into one of the large empty
waiting rooms looking for a pay phone.

Herschel Goodman was supposed to be spending a quiet
Sunday at home, but so far the effort had not been very
successful. His eldest son, David, was trying to build a soapbox
racer from instructions he had found in a library book, and
Goodman, much to his dismay, had been drafted to help. He
was not handy with tools. Unlike field archaeologists who could
carefully excavate the most delicate artifacts without damaging

91

them or reconstruct a priceless pottery vessel from hundreds of fragile shards, Herschel Goodman's talents were limited to analyzing data at the computer console. In contrast to his old friend Melville Dutton, Goodman could not fly an airplane, and even driving a car was a test of his coordination. Nevertheless many of the ideas Dutton had pursued so successfully were Goodman's. And as he worked on David's soapbox racer, Goodman was still turning over in his mind a new theory about a particularly puzzling set of four glyphs Mel had sent him just before his disappearance. A few bent nails and miscut boards later David finally agreed that he could probably do better on his own. Just then the phone rang.

Goodman was not entirely unprepared for the voice he heard. The last time he had seen Elaine Dutton, he had sensed that she and Dutton's family still had not accepted the fact of his death. After Liz's call he threw a parka over his jeans and workshirt and headed for his office at the university museum.

'He was there,' Liz said, as she returned to Holly. 'He's on his way to the museum now. He told me how to get there from here. It's not far at all.'

'We're going to set some kind of record this week,' said Holly with amusement, 'visiting closed museums.'

They followed Goodman's directions down Market to Thirty-third Street, then south to Spruce. The museum would be across from the stadium.

It was. Liz and Holly passed through the gate and found themselves in a quiet courtyard enclosed by ivy-covered brick walls.

'Beautiful,' said Holly. 'This looks very old. . .' She paused, blushing.

'I think you're beginning to feel at home in the twentieth century, Liz answered.

The guard at the desk inside knew who they were. 'Dr Goodman is expecting you. Come with me.' The girls followed him through the galleries past exhibit cases on either side.

'Look,' cried Holly suddenly. 'Maya things!' They had

entered a room full of stelae, all standing upright on low pedestals.

You're right, young lady,' allowed the guard. 'These are from Guatemala and Belize—and there's a big picture of the jungle they came from,' he added, pointing to the huge photograph that served as a backdrop.

'There's a temple from Tikal too,' said Liz, looking at another large photograph.

'You seem to know something about this stuff,' said the guard admiringly. 'You must have been doing a lot of reading.'

'Oh, some,' Holly boasted, looking over her shoulder at some jades in a glass case.

Quickly they crossed through what appeared to be a cafeteria built inside an enclosed bridge between two buildings. 'We'll soon be there,' said the guard, pressing the'up' button at a turn in the hallway beyond.

Goodman met them on the third floor and did his best to conceal his surprise as he ushered Liz and Holly to his office.

Mel Dutton's daughter wouldn't be very grown-up, of course, but he hadn't expected a couple of kids no older than his David. Assuming his most comforting manner, Goodman tried to answer their questions as well as he could.

'...Well, part of the proof is that the galaxies and the stars in the heavens are rushing away from one another at very fast speeds, hundreds of millions of miles an hour in some cases. So, if you trace this back in time, sort of like running a piece of movie film in reverse, you indeed discover that it comes together and begins twenty billion years ago.

'You see, girls, the Maya were obsessed with the past and also intensely curious about the future. They too tried to run their complicated calendar backward and even *forward* to predict future events...'

'I don't get it,' Liz said. 'How could a calendar foretell the future?'

'Well, it's like people today who believe in astrology. The Maya felt that the events of the heavens were related to events on Earth. They believed that history repeats itself and that

93

certain cycles of movements of stars and planets occurred at the same time as changes in their own realm—changes in dynasties, wars, religious events—even earthquakes. Most important, the Maya thought that the present cycle of history would end in the year we call A. D. 2013. At least that's the year according to the calendar correlation we use now, and radiocarbon dates seem to match up pretty well. According to their calculations—and not many would agree with me on this—we should now be entering a period of heavy earthquakes that will last until the cycles change again.

'This earthquake thing is most interesting to me. There's a particular glyphic symbol that Mel and I always thought actually meant "earthquake". It's an "earth" symbol, really, the *Caban* glyph that is one of the day names. But in some texts it's carved to look as if it were split—and it can't be the day sign in those texts. It's in the wrong position for a day sign. It's among the words that signify some kind of event, and it's just perfect for "earthquake." Mel called it the "cracked earth" glyph, and once he started looking for its occurrences in the inscriptions, he found more and more.

'When I was doing my postdoctoral research, I had the idea that it would be interesting to run some of these calendar predictions through the computer...to see if the Maya prophecies really had any basis in fact. One inscription that particularly interested me contained a time interval and a "cracked earth" glyph that worked out to an event that would happen early in our own month of February, 1976.'

Liz jumped. 'But there was a terrible earthquake about then! My dad was in the lowlands where the shocks weren't very strong, but I remember how worried we all were about him. In the mountains of Guatemala thousands of people died. Whole cities collapsed.'

Herschel Goodman shifted in his chair. 'That's right, Liz. Perhaps some of those lives could have been saved if anyone had taken my research seriously. But I'm afraid I can't blame them. Even I didn't believe that the earthquake would actually occur. Much of my idea was based on that strange glyph—that cracked earth glyph. Your father had more faith in my predictions than I did. He tried to convince the Guatemalan authorities to evacuate some of the highland towns, but, of course, they thought he was a madman...at the time.'

Professor Goodman looked so downcast that Liz felt eager to change the subject. 'How did you come to collaborate with my dad?' she asked.

'Well, that was very interesting in itself. On the basis of certain inscriptions that Mel had studied, he felt sure that he was on the track of a major new Maya ruin—a real lost city. You see, the Maya also used astronomical calculations and horizon sightings to determine the best locations for temples, religious sites, and cities. Mel felt that the inscriptions provided certain clues to such a location, and he wanted me to write a computer programme that would take account of all these clues and come up with a list of alignments that we could plot on satellite photographs to try to determine the location of the lost city.

'Working together benefited both of us,' Goodman went on. 'Mel had reason to believe that this city would contain new stelae, unlooted tombs, or perhaps even hieroglyphic manuscripts that survived the centuries and the Spanish conquest as well. If so, that would have given me many more detailed predictions to study. My computer calculations would have made it possible for Mel to locate his city in the first place. As you must know, Liz, archaeological expeditions and preliminary digs cost thousands of dollars. Even considering Mel's reputation for lucky finds, no one was eager to advance him that kind of money just to go poking around in the jungle, looking for a lost city. Many mesoamerican specialists resented your father's theories, I'm afraid. There was some feeling that your father's expeditions were diverting funds from other worthy projects. Some even said he had a bit of gold fever...and was following Cortes's 1525 route searching for treasure. Nonsense, of course.'

'But what happened?' Liz asked impatiently. 'Did you figure out where Dad's city might be?'

Once again Herschel Goodman looked uneasy. 'No, Liz. We quarrelled.'

'Why?'

'Well, the satellite photos we needed to complete the calculations aren't going to be released by the United States and Guatemalan governments for three more years. The real purpose for taking them was military intelligence. I was doing some work for NASA and had access to the photos, but not for any private investigation. I simply couldn't violate my oath of confidentiality. Your father was impatient and thought me unnecessarily cautious, since he certainly wasn't going to use them for any hostile purposes. He kept worrying about delay and about looters and art thieves who are so active in Guatemala. Your father had already had one painful experience with them, I believe.'

'Yes,' Liz answered. 'He discovered some kind of statue and then when he went back to study it again several years later, it was gone.'

'That's right,' said Goodman. 'That was the only life-sized Maya statue ever found in place in a cave shrine, too. And now it's disappeared, most probably cut up and sold in sections to some collector who doesn't care about its scientific importance or how he got great works of art—so long as they're unusual...and expensive.

'At any rate, when Sean Wilkins offered to finance your father's next expedition, he decided not to wait for my final calculations, but to chance it on what he had. I thought he was making a big mistake.'

Goodman was interrupted by the arrival of a strikingly handsome young man wearing an embroidered shirt.

'This is Felipe Sánchez,' Goodman said. 'He worked with your father at Tikal, Liz, and I'm sure he would like to meet you and your friend.'

'It's an honour, senoritas,' Felipe said, bowing.

'Felipe is here to see about getting on to another expedition in the Maya area,' explained Goodman. 'I guess working with Mel Dutton in the ruins has gotten into his blood.'

'Professor Dutton was a very dedicated man, and a courageous one,' continued Felipe. 'He believed there was nothing he could not accomplish and nothing he could not

96

learn. The study of the Maya was like a first love for him. He felt no danger.'

Holly had been unusually quiet throughout Professor Goodman's long explanations, but when Sánchez finished, she broke into an odd singsong recitation:

'First love is like a dream begotten;
The words it speaks are ne'er forgotten;
There is much the mind cannot recall;
But the heart's diary remembers all.'

'Sí, sí, the diary of the heart senorita. Very poetic,' said Felipe.

But the expression on Holly's face was anything but dreamy. 'Didn't Mel Dutton keep a diary, Professor Goodman?' asked Holly suddenly. 'He always did as a child, I distinctly remember that now.'

Goodman looked perplexed, and Liz shook her head at Holly in warning.

'I mean, Mrs Agatha Dutton, Mel's mother, showed them to me,' Holly said, correcting herself hastily.

Liz sighed.

'Oh, yes, naturally Mel kept field notes. But I wouldn't have them. Some of his notebooks would be on loan to the Smithsonian Institute in Washington, D. C. There is some sort of arrangement, I understand, to hold a posthumous exhibition there of photos from Mel's last expedition.'

Liz looked disturbed, but Holly spoke up decisively. 'Thank you very much, Professor. I am afraid we must take leave of you. now.'

'Just a second, girls. I can't let Mel Dutton's daughter and her friend leave Philadelphia without at least inviting you to dinner. In fact, you must stay the night. I'm sure your mothers would want it that way.' Goodman looked at them carefully. 'They do know where you are, don't they?'

'Oh, yes, of course she knows,' Liz replied too quickly. 'I mean *they* know...both our mothers.'

'Well, then, we can just drive right over to the house. You

97

can meet my family. Then tonight we can call your mother, Liz.'

Goodman shoved aside the mound of computer printouts that littered his desk and retrieved his parka, which had been lying in a heap on the floor. As he strode through the outer office on his way to get the station wagon from the parking lot, Liz and Holly heard him whisper instructions to Felipe. It was all very casual, but it almost seemed as if Goodman wanted his assistant to keep an eye on them. There was no chance of their slipping away.

'This is terrible,' Liz moaned. 'We've got to go to Washington. You heard what he said about the diary.'

'You need not worry,' Holly said, unperturbed. 'Sunday is a day of rest. Maybe Professor Goodman is trying to distract us. Let us make ample use of his telephone and find out more about his calculations.'

'Two days ago you didn't even know how a phone worked,' Liz said in amazement. 'Now you come up with a scheme like that. You really have nerve, Holly.'

Unsure of whether to be offended or pleased, Holly winked mischievously. Then, abruptly, she turned serious again. 'I suspect that Professor Goodman was not entirely forthright with us when he told about his quarrel with your father. Perhaps he, too, was envious of your father's success.'

The idea that her father was not popular among his fellow archaeologists bothered Liz a lot. She had heard her father talk about debates with his colleagues over one theory or another, but to her, Mel Dutton was a hero, a celebrity with his picture in magazines. For the first time Liz realized that his flair for getting publicity might make enemies too.

'Liz, Liz. I'm home!'

'Where shall I put the presents for the children?' Hal Abbot asked loudly, following Elaine into her apartment, a suitcase in each hand. Elaine waved her hand vaguely in the direction of the living room and went in to wake her daughter. A few seconds later she emerged, puzzled and worried. 'Hal, they're not here. Two beds have been slept in, so Liz and her friend must have arrived. I don't understand where they could be.'

'Maybe they just went to the movies.'

'It's after midnight. Young teenagers don't go to the movies at this time of night, not my thirteen-year-old, anyway.'

'In that case perhaps we should call the police.'

Hal moved decisively towards the phone, but it rang before he could lift the receiver.

'That must be Liz now,' Elaine said, grabbing the phone from Hal's hands. 'Oh, Danny, it's you? Where's Liz?... Philadelphia??... Professor Herschel Goodman's house?... Yes, I'm sorry. I was late getting back from Washington. We'll have to check the Goodmans tomorrow...You say you're going to be on the early bus tomorrow? Great, I'll meet you at the Port Authority station...'

'What is Liz doing in Philadelphia? Hal asked as Elaine hung up the phone indignantly.

'I have a feeling it's a long story,' said Elaine, resigned to the matter. 'You'd better go now, Hal. I appreciate your meeting my plane, but I have a big day tomorrow. I have to pick Danny up at lunchtime and probably go back for Liz later.'

'That's all right. I can pick Danny up. Can't I at least buy you a brandy or a cup of coffee?'

'I'm afraid I'm just too tired—and frankly too worried about Liz—to be sociable tonight. Thanks again for helping me, and I'll see you tomorrow.'

Defeated, he picked up his coat. 'If that little brat were my daughter...' he muttered to himself as he went down in the elevator.

Monday, November 27

Liz was elated by the way things had worked out the evening before. The Goodmans had gone to bed without being able to reach her mother. But now it was important to get out of the house before the Goodmans woke up. She woke Holly who headed off to the bathroom, an expert now on what she called the 'inhouse.' The girls were as quiet as they could be as they made their way down the front stairs.

When they were safely out the front door, Liz suggested they go somewhere for breakfast and wait until John Wanamaker's opened.

'Is Wanamaker's still another museum?' Holly asked.

'No, it's a department store. I think we need some more supplies and real suitcases.'

'Perhaps we do need more provisions,' Holly agreed as she looked down at her carpetbag. 'Every leg of our journey seems to be taking us farther and farther away from your home.'

The luggage department had every type of carrying device imaginable in it, from hand-tote bags with a single zipper to monstrous travel bags bristling with buttons, zippers, and secret compartments. Liz began looking closely at a small suitcase with a tartan pattern, while Holly was collared by a salesman.

'This thrilling bag can carry *all* your dresses! And there are pockets within pockets within pockets, so you can keep all your favourite perfumes at hand's reach!'

The salesman leaned towards Holly conspiratorially and spoke in a whisper. 'And there are secret places for money, lipstick, eyelashes...boyfriends' letters...you can carry *anything,* anything at all in this marvel of a bag!'

Holly looked around desperately for a means of escape from the salesman and spotted just what she needed.

Liz paid the clerk for her suitcase, and the saleswoman adjusted her spectacles to read the name off the credit card. 'This is John Wanamaker's, she explained, 'and in John Wanamaker's everything has been done in triplicate since before they invented electronic calculators.'

Liz left the counter and went to go rescue Holly from the salesman. But Holly seemed to have vanished.

'Where's my friend?' Liz cried in alarm. 'Holly!' She ran up to the salesman. 'What happened to my friend?'

'Well, I...I don't know.' He scanned the room once, trying to be helpful. 'She just disappeared in thin air.'

'I've got to find her!'

'I don't suppose she could have gone too far.'

'You don't know Holly. She could have gone a *long* way.'

Liz led the man frantically around the room, looking behind every counter and bag. Finally, as they came up to where the clothing bags were hanging, the zipper on one of them began moving by itself. Suddenly out dropped Holly.

'Quite spacious, actually,' Holly said, with a little curtsy.

The Metroliner to Washington, D. C., pulled in on time, and Holly and Liz clambered their way through the commuters to get a seat. they sat by a well-groomed man in a black pinstripe suit. Everybody around them seemed to have a briefcase or an attaché case. Suddenly a man sitting behind them leaned over their seat. 'Do you think your hearings will

101

get to the bottom of this illegal alien business, Senator?' he said to the man in the pinstripe suit. The senator was so engrossed in his book he didn't even seem to hear the inquiry.

'Excuse me, sir,' Holly said. 'What is it that you are working on?'

With a self-important flourish he stated, 'I'm charged with the responsibility of overseeing the protection of our borders.'

The senator returned to his book. Holly tipped forward and peeked at the cover. Then she leaned over and whispered in Liz's ear. 'It says *Professional Makeup and Dress for Television.*'

The Metroliner delivered Liz and Holly promptly at one-thirty to Washington's Union Station. Holly by now saw ironically that 'rush hour' was that hour when traffic was at a standstill, and began to understand that people did not lie down in rest rooms and that a loudspeaker was not a town crier. The girls paused to buy a map of the city and boarded the subway beneath the station, and successfully changed trains at Metro Center. A few minutes later a sonorous voice announced, 'Next stop, Smithsonian.' The long escalator pointed them to the light above, and they emerged, elated, in the middle of the Mall.

For Washington it was a splendid day. The air was crisp and invigorating. The city had escaped the Thanksgiving snowstorm, and the smooth lawn that stretched toward the Washington Monument lay as clean as an untrodden meadow of grey-green. The dome of the Capitol building rode high on the opposite horizon, gleaming in the brilliant sun of early afternoon.

'What a beautiful place,' said Holly, pleased, 'but what in the world is *that*?' 'she asked, gazing at the huge white obelisk that dominated the open area where they stood.

'That, my friend,' replied Liz, 'is the Washington Monument. You remember George, of course,' she added slyly.

'Yes, I do, though he died when I was just nine. He was a good president, and it is nice he has such a big gravestone.'

'He's not buried there,' said Liz. 'It's just a monument to him. Doesn't it make you feel weird to see something like that, a memorial to someone who was alive when you were—I mean, when you were alive for the first time?'

'Some,' Holly said abstractly. 'I feel somewhat sad. But it's wonderful to see that the old presidents are still remembered.'

They were approaching a massive domed building that lay along one side of the Mall.

'That's got to be the Natural History Museum,' said Liz, pausing to look carefully at the map. 'Yes. That's the Old Smithsonian behind us, that red brick thing that looks like a castle.'

'Old?' said Holly looking back. 'It doesn't look very old to *me*.'

'Never mind,' Liz said with a touch of exasperation. 'We've found the building where Dr Goodman said the exhibit of Dad's photographs is being set up. Here's the name of the man we're supposed to talk to, Clive Witherspoon.'

The uniformed guard called Witherspoon for them. 'He's here and you can see him,' he told the girls. 'Go get your visitors' passes there,' he added, pointing to a small office door. 'Then take the elevator to three. Mr Witherspoon will meet you.'

The elevator door opened on a long hallway narrowed by grey wooden cabinets along one side. Atop them lay old baskets and busts of Indians who glared silently at the opposite wall.

Clive Witherspoon, a tall, thin man with white hair and a tattered green sweater that only seemed to magnify his distinguished appearance, stepped towards them.

'Greetings, girls,' he said graciously. 'Welcome to a part of the Smithsonian that not very many people see—in many ways it's more interesting than the exhibits downstairs,' he added smiling. 'I'll have to ask you to bear with me. We're in the middle of putting up the exhibit of your father's photographs, Miss Elizabeth, so I'll take you there.' He led them down the hall past still more cabinets, and they took another elevator back to the second floor. It opened on what appeared to be a carpentry shop. The whine of a saw stopped abruptly, and two workmen moved a huge sheet of plywood to an area where others were painting the newly mounted panels.

'Careful of all the wires on the floor,' cautioned Witherspoon. 'We've come into the exhibit the back way. In a

103

few days it will be opened, and all this stuff will be out of the way. No one ever really knows how much work these things take.'

Clive Witherspoon clearly relished the prospect of giving guided tours. He ushered the girls into a side room where enormous photo blowups leaned against the wall. One drew Liz immediately to it. It showed Mel Dutton in khakis, high boots, and the familiar straw hat. Dutton stood with one hand resting on a giant stela that leaned sharply, as if ready to fall. Behind him rose what appeared to be the biggest tree in the world. Liz regarded the picture solemnly. The idea of everyone in Washington looking at a picture of her dad taken after she had last seen him left her with a dull pang of grief, but Holly seemed fascinated.

'My goodness,' she exclaimed. 'This is even better than that *People* cover in his old room.'

'Why, thank you, young lady. Now if you all will just step over this way...'

'...A basic requirement of this particular expedition was endurance,' Witherspoon said, pointing to a larger-than-life photo of Dutton doing push-ups. 'The natives thought we were crazy...but your dad explained away these push-ups as a strange eastern religious exercise.'

Liz remembered the way Holly had exercised upon emerging from the picture. It occurred to Liz that physical fitness must be a family trait.

'Tell me, Mr Witherspoon,' Holly asked. 'Why was Professor Dutton so interested in a country full of heathens?'

For the first time, the courtly gentleman looked at a loss for words, but he recovered quickly. 'The saga of the Maya is a very fascinating thing,' he said reflectively. 'I know many people who study them. They all wonder, of course, what caused them to be like they were or why their civilization declined—things like that are not easy to answer. There's something about the area, too. I've heard it said by many that once one goes into the Petén jungle, his life can never again be the same...there's definitely something about it. You know, we're not even sure where the Maya came from.'

'But I know where I came from,' Holly interrupted. 'I am descended from the Pilgrims.'

'Yes, that's interesting. You know, you might say that, in a way, Mel Dutton was a modern-day pilgrim—one who walked back into time...'

Holly looked at the old man with new respect, but Liz was less impressed.

'Tell me, sir, why did the Smithsonian abandon my father last March?'

'Abandon him?' Witherspoon seemed genuinely surprised. 'That's perhaps too strong a term. We didn't abandon him. Our concession, our legal government exploration permit expired, that's all. Perhaps if your father had been content to stay at Tikal, we could have arranged to continue the support of his work. As much as I respected his goals, I'm afraid that his insistence on wandering off into the jungle for weeks at a time was simply too vague a plan for both us and the Guatemalans. Your father seemed convinced he was on the track of a major ruined city, as large or larger than Tikal, that lay out there somewhere. Intriguing, yes, but also a gamble and, as Sean Wilkins has assured us, a most unlikely prospect.'

'Mr Witherspoon,' Liz asked carefully. 'Could I, could we see Dad's last diary—the one Professor Goodman says you brought back in March?'

'Of course, Miss Elizabeth. It's back up on my desk. Come.'

The three sat in Witherspoon's crowded office. The old man apologized for the litter, then retrieved the diary from beneath a stack of acquisition forms on top of which a Styrofoam cup of cold coffee had sat precariously.

Liz and Holly pulled their chairs together and read the now familiar handwriting of Mel Dutton:

Tikal, Guatemala, March 15

Survival in this dense jungle is a matter of sheer endurance. I begin, though, to sense some of the pride that Morley, Schliemann, Leakey, and others must have felt, and it drives me on. But often my intellect and senses seem dulled by the sun — like a rapture of the deep. A longer stay might be fatal. My mind wanders, and for the first time I am afraid — afraid more of failure than of death

The jade pendant that I'm going to send Liz is a magnificent piece. Too bad I don't know where it was found, but if that had been known, it is doubtful that the Guatemalan government would have presented it to me. I have drawn it carefully in the event it gets lost, for I feel it is somehow important to my quest in this rain forest.

The pendant is 3¾" wide, 2⅝" high, and

barely ½" thick. The front is carved into a jaguar profile with a plant attached. The back bears the following glyphs:

9 Kan
→

17 Ceh
←

VENUS EVENT (?).
→

"Jaguar City" (?)

Now, the latest discovery: All my searching in the immediate vicinity of Temple IV has paid off. God knows why the stela fragment was not seen before! I suppose because no one was specifically looking for it. Only a fragment but, for once, the _right_ piece.

This new fragment bears the Maya calendar round date 6 Kan 17 Chen — the end of a Long Count date that, though mostly missing, HAS to be 9.17.14.12.4 — nothing else can possibly work. ↓

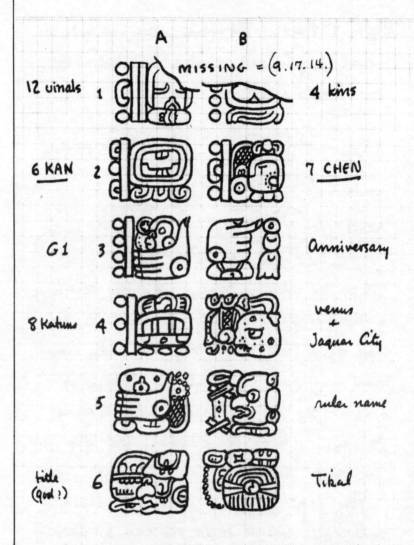

	A	B	
		MISSING = (9.17.14.)	
12 uinals	1		4 kins
6 KAN	2		7 CHEN
G1	3		Anniversary
8 Katuns	4		venus + Jaguar City
	5		ruler name
title (god?)	6		Tikal

It is also stated in the inscription (at B3
and A4, above) that the date 9.17.14.12.4
is the 8th Katun anniversary of another

date. By subtracting, we get:

Stela date = 9. 17. 14. 12. 4   6 kan 7 Chen

minus _____ 8. 0. 0. 0

(Oct 28, 627) = 9. 9. 14. 12. 4   9 kan 17 Ceh

→ This day, 9 kan 17 Ceh is the same as that on the pendant. We therefore have correspondence of **date** + **event** + **Jaguar City** between the pendant and the stela! What in the world can it mean???

SPECULATION: We think that virtually no stelae were erected at Tikal between about A.D. 600 + 700 (except for Stela 40). Could one of Tikal's rulers have abdicated the rulership and left, perhaps to establish a new capital for his dynasty? Could **that** be the "Jaguar City"? We know that place —wherever it is— relates to Tikal, but is **not** Tikal. And the Maya are trying to tell me that Venus has something to do with the answer!

Funds are now running out, yet I am reluctant to leave this mystery behind me. I was 43 years old last month, and no longer do I feel as I once did – that there will always be another season's exploration – another opportunity in which to make the discovery of a lifetime. Money is scarcer now than it's ever been and vandals are at work, even in the most remote areas of Petén. I feel that if this stela and the pendant are leading me to some other site, some treasury of information, I must find it while there is still time.

I have spent three years now studying Temple IV, and in my imagination I can almost see the incredible ceremonies that were held in the plaza here during the heyday of Tikal. I doubt that the Maya of those times could have conceived of an age when their great city would lie deserted, the music and noise of that time stilled forever.

But I wonder sometimes, on evenings like this one, when our work crew is gathered around the campfire and one of the men is playing on a little flute, whether my spirit has passed into a time long gone — one of crowds and quetzal plumes, and brightly painted stone buildings. The Maya are not really dead — this is a conceit of men like me who have come to place more importance in mute stones than in human souls. I wonder if Liz and Danny would be able to understand any of this. Will they, or Elaine, ever be able to forgive me for spending so much of my life in this jungle?

———

Liz silently closed the battered book, placed it on the edge of the desk, and touched her pendant lovingly. 'He *did* care so much for us, Holly.' Liz flushed momentarily, realizing that now even she was thinking of her father in the past tense. 'I'm just now beginning to realize what he must have gone through, trying not to be lonely, but still wanting to be in that jungle.'

Holly turned to Witherspoon. 'Could you tell me, sir,' she asked, 'if there might not be later diary entries?'

'None that we know of, my dear. Oh, incidentally, Liz, how would you like to meet Mr Sean Wilkins, your dad's ex-partner? Actually he's here now, in the building,' Witherspoon explained, leaning towards Liz and Holly and speaking carefully. 'Wilkins is an archaeologist of sorts, but, as he himself says, more of an art historian. He was, I believe, the curator of a small museum somewhere in California. Egyptology is his first field, but he's into everything now—particularly the art of the Maya. Now he runs ICAR, the Institute for Central American Research, in New Orleans.'

Now Witherspoon spoke even more cautiously. 'You should know this about the man though if you ever say I told you this, I will deny it,' he cautioned with a slight smile. 'I'm afraid that Wilkins is known more as an ''operator'' than an archaeologist or art historian. He is famous for his ability to attract wealthy patrons and really unknown for any scholarship or publications. There's a good deal of ill feeling between Wilkins and scholars in general, and *that* is why you may have gathered that Professor Goodman did *not* approve of your father's decision to accept some sponsor money from Wilkins. We are partially at fault there; we put Wilkins in touch with your father when it became clear that our permits would expire. We thought that Wilkins could help. Wilkins works for insurance companies as an art detective and appraiser. People like him are much sought after. You see, stolen and looted artifacts are now ranked criminally second only to narcotics traffic internationally. Wilkins seems to have *connections* everywhere, even in Guatemala. And no one can deny that Wilkins knows his Maya art. That's what he's here for today. We asked him to look over our old Maya collections to authenticate certain pieces and, perhaps, to suggest where they may have come from. Many of the old labels are unreadable now, or else the specimens came through donations. Anyway, you should meet him; that is, if you'd like to.'

'Surely we would,' Holly replied eagerly.

As the girls followed Witherspoon back through the long hallway, Liz tried to remember what she had heard about Wilkins from her parents. Elaine had met him when she went down to Petén at the time of the search. Her mother, Liz recalled, had been impressed with Wilkins's concern, commenting in one of her letters that Wilkins seemed almost as worried and anxious as she was. Clive Witherspoon, on the other hand, seemed to assume that Liz had heard bad things about her father's last partner.

Still turning these contradictions over in her mind, Liz followed Witherspoon and Holly into a large room where two museum assistants were going through the deep drawers of a tall storage cabinet. Some vases were laid out on a table where a fashionably dressed man in his mid-thirties sat writing in a notebook. Liz recognized the man as Wilkins immediately, remembering her mother's descriptions of the charming British accent and elegant manner that made such an impression on the wealthy visitors at the Tikal site. Elaine had been very approving. Wilkins seemed particularly good at impressing possible patrons.

Now, as Clive Witherspoon introduced Liz and Holly, Holly suddenly wondered whether Wilkins was indeed as pleased to see them as he outwardly appeared.

'I wish, dears, that we had some clue as to what happened to Mel Dutton. But I'm afraid,' he added, turning to address Liz directly, 'that you've travelled all this way for nothing. Your mother and I searched the camp thoroughly in July. The diaries we turned in to Mr Witherspoon here were the last Mel wrote before he departed on his ill-advised venture into the jungle. He left in mid-March and was never seen again, so, of course, there was no later communication. I fear that the letters and tape-recorded greetings Mel left me to fly out when I departed on March seventeenth were the last words anyone will ever hear from Mel Dutton. A great pity. It must be very difficult for you.'

'Tape?' Liz wondered out loud. 'There was no tape. But Daddy did send me this pendant and a letter wrapped inside the plastic cassette container. That must be what you saw.' With studied casualness Liz pulled out the jade pendant she was wearing under her shirt.

The flicker of exitement that crossed Wilkins's face lasted just an instant. 'How nice that you have a momento of your father,' he said.'

'Do you know what kind of animal this could be?' Holly asked innocently. 'It looks like some kind of cat to me.'

'It is a jaguar, of course. The whole symbol is a glyph in the Maya writing system. I don't recognize this particular one offhand, but I doubt that the carving itself is of much value. Other than the sentimental, of course. Why don't you let me sent it on to one of my research assistants, and he can return it to you with a complete report on its significance?'

Liz hesitated as Wilkins reached for the pendant, then, slowly, placed the charm back inside her shirt.

'I'm sorry, but no. As much as I'd like to know about the jaguar, I don't want to part with it, even temporarily.'

'I see. In that case I'm sorry that I can't be more helpful. Please give my best regards to your mother and remind her that whenever she has time to visit us in New Orleans, we'll be happy to see her.' Wilkins turned back to the table.

'One sprinkles the most sugar where the tart is burnt,' said Holly as they walked away. 'I don't trust that man at all. He bears some looking into. I think *we* should pay him a visit.'

Liz agreed that she and Holly would have to investigate this man further.

*L*ater that same afternoon in New York Elaine Dutton went with Hal Abbot to meet Danny at the Port Authority bus station. She was nervous enough already about the way things were going—the call from the Goodmans informing her of Liz's premature departure (with a girl friend she'd picked up from God knows where) was still fresh in her mind—and it didn't help matters when she couldn't find Danny where the passengers were supposed to have disembarked.

Finally, with the help of a porter, she discovered him in the baggage department, along with three other children under twelve who had travelled alone. All of them had small square tags on their chests, and Danny's said in big, bold red letters: 'I am Danny.' The small blond-haired boy beside him was wailing at the top of his lungs, 'I'm not a package!' Danny was regarding the whole humiliating experience with what seemed to be an ironic little scowl.

But when Elaine got him away from there, it turned out he

hadn't taken the experience so lightly after all. He was unusually quiet the entire trip home, especially about his sister. Elaine realized that she was unlikely to pry much information from Danny as long as Hal was present, but the boy had already missed the morning session of his school because she hadn't wanted him to travel alone at night, and now she didn't want him to miss his afternoon classes as well. So Hal drove Danny to his private school, while Elaine went along with them. On the trip back to the office Elaine hoped that Liz and her friend would be home that evening, and then both would have some heavy explaining to do. But meanwhile she worried. She would try to concentrate on Hal's latest marketing theories.

He started in the moment they reached Elaine's executive suite at Reynolds Publishing.

'Our point-of-purchase research shows that magenta and black move books off the shelves better than any other colour combination,' Hal said, as he spread out a display of sample book jackets on a small conference table. 'Photos have a positive effect for nonfiction, but their impact on the sale of novels is negligible...'He paused in mid-sentence to study Elaine's face. 'I'm sorry. I realize you're worried about Liz. But I have to have your ideas for the art work by the end of the week. You can't let the children interfere with your professional life to this degree.'

'The children *are* my life, Hal. I suppose you think your studies on why Scarsdale housewives buy magenta books as opposed to yellow-green ones really turn me on, but they don't...'

'All right, all right. You know I'm concerned too. It's just that you're not going to solve Liz's problems by becoming a nervous wreck yourself. I suggest that Liz's 'ancestral' travelling companion may be imaginary, and that you should take Liz to a psychiatrist pronto. These delusions aren't uncommon, considering the strain she's been under, but you can't hope to deal with it yourself.'

'But there were two beds slept in...You saw it.'

'Elaine, Liz could have used both beds herself. That's not

116

evidence. We have no way of knowing that there was another girl with Liz.'

'Agatha didn't say this Holly what's-her-name was a delusion. She was almost as vague about the whole thing as Danny was...Excuse me...this could be important.'

Hal grimaced helplessly as Elaine picked up the phone and assumed her most ingratiating tone of voice for the benefit of whoever was on the line. 'Why, of course, Clive, delighted to hear from you. 'I've been looking forward to seeing you at the exhibit opening...Washington is more exciting than New York these days it seems...She did! You say Liz dropped in with a friend of hers? A friend slightly older than she?...Yes...Yes...Yes, of course. Thank you so much for letting me know that they got a chance to drop by. I'm sure they're heading home. 'Bye now.

'Did you hear that, Hal?' said Elaine. 'It appears that Liz's friend isn't a delusion after all.'

'That remains to be discovered,' Hal said crisply. 'Remember, many cases of multiple personalities have been able to convince others that their alter egos actually exist. The girl your Washington friend saw could have been someone Liz picked up anywhere, to prove her existence. And shouldn't Liz—or they—have returned by now?'

'I hadn't even thought about that yet. I wonder if they've gotten into some trouble.'

'If you don't mind my intruding on your *personal* concerns,' Hal said acidly, 'I have a suggestion. I'll go back and stake out the bus station just in case Liz does happen to appear there. In the meantime I'm going to call Jed Barnstable. He's a child psychologist, one of the best in the business, and he happens to be an old classmate of mine as well. Princeton, class of fifty-five. I think, as a favour to me, Jed would agree to drop in at your apartment late this afternoon. I'm sure he would know the best way to proceed from here.'

'But if Liz is in trouble, we can't afford to waste time,' Elaine pressed.

'Whatever Liz's problems may be, incompetence at making travelling arrangements doesn't seem to be one of them. Not at least when you so thoughtfully provided her with unlimited credit.'

Unaware that by the time the afternoon ended he would have his first meeting with a child psychologist, Danny Dutton was sprawled across his bed, munching crisps and studying his collection of air timetables. For all of Hal Abbot's sarcasm, it was Danny, not Liz, who was the real genius in the family when it came to planning, and not five minutes earlier his sister had called from Washington to ask his advice on getting to New Orleans.

The solitary bus ride from Sturbridge had given Danny plenty of time to regret his passive role in Liz's plans, and so, given this important role to play, Danny had performed above and beyond the call of duty. Realizing that Liz's credit cards and letters might not cut much ice with the airline personnel, Danny had volunteered his impressive vocabulary and foghorn voice. In short order 'Dr Daniel Dutton' had made reservations with Eastern Airlines for his 'teenage' sisters, who would, due to a family emergency, be flying unaccompanied from Washington to New Orleans. then the same 'Dr Dutton' called the Hotel Monteleone, where his mother and father had stayed during their visits to Wilkins's institute, and informed the desk clerk that Miss Elizabeth Dutton and her cousin would be arriving that evening, a day in advance of himself and his mother, and could the hotel arrange for its limousine to pick the girls up at the airport?

Liz, informed by return call of her brother's success, was for once properly appreciative. 'The only thing that bothers me, Danny, is what will happen when Mum and Dr Daniel Dutton never show up at the hotel?'

'Don't worry about that problem,' Danny had assured her. 'I'm quite sure we *will* be there by tomorrow evening. I can't keep lying to Mum forever. It wouldn't be fair. The way I figure it, you have one day in New Orleans on your own, so make the best of it.'

'But, Liz,' Danny added, crunching another crisp, 'what have you found out?...No kidding?...You mean Wilkins

118

didn't know about Dad's letter? Unreal!'

'Right. Wilkins thought he was just sending Dad's tapes, and he never even knew that the letter and the pendant were inside the cassette container. And what's more, he said he flew Dad's letters out on the seventeenth, but the letter was dated the twenty-second.'

'I wonder why Wilkins lied. Maybe Dad *is* alive after all! Maybe you've been right all along! Maybe he's alive and for some reason Wilkins doesn't want anybody to know it! Alive! Wow! I've never really let myself believe. . . What's that? Your friend Holly wants to give me a message? Say it again. 'Where folks believe in witches, witches are; but when they don't believe, there are none there.' Thanks a lot, Liz. Yeah, I know you don't understand it, but I do. Look, I'm signing off now. I'm really with you *both*. So long.'

Danny was not pleased by the arrival at five o'clock of Dr Jed Barnstable. Sizing up their visitor as bright but humourless, Danny seized the chance to control the conversation. After all, he figured, any friend of Hal Abbot's was fair game. Danny shook Dr Barnstable's hand and gave a loud sigh before answering the doctor's supposedly innocent question about whether Liz had appeared to be enjoying the weekend at Sturbridge. Ten minutes later he was still talking like a tape on a machine:

'. . . Dr Jung might have disagreed with Dr Freud. He probably would have referred to Liz's friend's sudden appearance as hyperevoc. . . evocation. Now Mum's problem is basically that she edits all those books on parapsychology and the supernatural. Y'know, kids that are called 'things,' and exorcisms of girls who use filthy language. Personally I have yet to meet a girl who can't outswear any boy in her class. But I definitely saw her, if that's what you want to know.'

'Saw who?' Dr Barnstable asked brightly, eager to take credit for Danny's return to a relevant train of thought.

'Well, it was early in the morning, y'know. I was still pretty sleepy. I'd been having a very interesting dream. . .'

'Danny, get to the point!' Elaine warned.

'As I was saying, she was no kid I ever saw before. Liz called her Lolly Hobbie...or maybe it was Holly Lobbie. But she was definitely palpable. Very nicely built for her age, if you know what I mean.'

'It is necessary for children to have certain escape hatches,' said Dr Barnstable, addressing Elaine Dutton as though Danny were not present. 'Hope itself is a form of escape hatch. But we must distinguish between hope and hallucination. Of course it's possible that the problem is deeper than mere childish wish fulfillment. Your daughter may have projected onto her companion—*if* she really exists at all—one facet of her own fragmented identity. In fact, fully developed multiple personalities are more common in popular literature than they are in clinical practice, but they do exist. Naturally I'm just speculating. A third and more noncommittal position—the one I favour, incidentally—is that your daughter is suffering from a temporary psychosis brought on by her inability to accept the facts of your husband's disappearance. I think Danny here knows very well that there is no such person as this girl Holly, but he wants to defend his sister and to find a rational explanation for her actions...'

'I suppose I could have seen an aura and not a real girl,' Danny said, pretending to accept this judgement. 'There are *reputable* specialists who believe in the appearance of emanations. The Russians call them by the technical name 'bioplasma,' which they demonstrate through their expertise in Kirlian photography.'

'Bioplasma—sounds like a great one-word book title to me,' mused Elaine.

The sarcasm in her voice did not escape the good doctor, and he began to show his irritation. 'Mrs Dutton, we don't appear to be entirely serious here, do we?' Dr Barnstable scolded, trying to maintain his professional tone. Then, turning to Danny in all earnestness, he asked, 'Did Liz claim that her little friend was clairvoyant?'

'Claire Voyant?' drawled Danny, twirling an imaginary cigar and batting his eyes in what he believed to be a fair Groucho Marx imitation. 'No...Holly Hobbie!'

'I'm sorry to have wasted your time, Dr Barnstable,' said

120

Elaine. And the psychiatrist, who had indeed begun to glance apprehensively at his watch, was now only a shade away from exploding. Grabbing his briefcase and coat, he hurried angrily out the door while Elaine Dutton fell on the couch in a fit of giggles. 'Danny, you were absolutely wonderful,' she gasped at last. 'Now, you'd better level with me or I'll condemn you to see that man twice a week until you're sixteen! Where's Liz?'

*D*warfed by the immense curving sweep of the concrete roof that seemed to soar above them, Liz and Holly stood near the departure gate of Dulles International Airport. Of all the buildings that Holly had seen during these incredible few days, this had impressed her the most.

'Like a ship on the sea,' she had murmured in awe as the bus topped the final crest on the airport access highway, revealing the lone building in the midst of a vast plain. The sun of late afternoon, at that moment, peeped through a massive cloud bank on the western horizon, only to be caught by the glass of the distant control tower and reflected into the bus. 'I almost wish it *were* a ship,' added Holly more loudly, to the amusement of the fellow passengers in the surrounding seats. 'Will I be frightened by the airship, Liz?'

'Not you, my friend,' Liz had replied. 'Remember the Eleventh Commandment—"Though shalt maintain thy cool." '

'Eastern flight 553 to New Orleans is now ready for boarding

122

through gate three,' said a voice that filled the terminal with astounding clarity.

Holly Hobbie, at last about to have her chance to fly, began moving with Liz and the line into the mobile lounge—the waiting room on wheels that would take them to the airplane. By now Holly realized that it was not necessary to set traps to catch buses, trains, and planes. The girls found two seats opposite the end they had entered. 'If we sit here,' Liz said with the authority of long experience at such things, 'we can get out first.'

Under the careful manipulation of the uniformed driver, the great metal box detached itself from the terminal-building door, lowered like a great accordion onto its massive chassis, backed off, turned, and lumbered slowly toward the distant runway. Soon the low rectangles of the Eastern maintenance shops appeared in the lounge window and then the giant L-1011.

'I tell you, Holly, it just doesn't make sense to me . . .' Liz began.

'I echo your sentiments,' interrupted Holly, looking almost directly upward at the enormous aircraft. 'I thought that airships would be light and graceful, like birds. This appears much too heavy to fly . . . It is taller than the church in Sturbridge.'

'I'm not talking about the plane. I'm trying to figure out our conversation with Wilkins. He said that the personal effects and papers he and Mother found in Dad's tent were the last things of Dad's ever discovered. He also said that on March seventeenth he flew to New Orleans and that he didn't see Dad any more after that.'

'But your dad's letter which Wilkins gave your mother for you was dated March twenty-second! Something is not right, as Danny said on the phone! Who knows, maybe Wilkins has even later diaries or letters of your father's hidden around his institute. That is what we have to look for in New Orleans,' Holly said.

'Speaking of the devil!' Liz suddenly exclaimed. 'Do you see who I see?' She nodded toward the distant end of the mobile lounge as everyone began to rise, for the doorway near them had now risen and joined the side door of the airplane. Sean Wilkins was hurriedly checking the contents of his green suede attaché case. 'We can ask him ourselves.'

Holly clapped her hand over Liz's mouth and pulled her out of sight. 'If there is anything odd about Wilkins's story, we ought to have a better plan than just asking him. Then, too, I suspect he will not be pleased to know that we are following him.

'But how can we possibly get on the plane without his seeing us?'

Not knowing what else to do, the girls quickly moved into the plane, smiling calmly as the stewardess tore off the stubs of their boarding passes. 'Your seats are in the back, down the far aisle and by the window on the left.'

'Very well,' said Liz with a glance over her shoulder, hoping that Wilkins was travelling first class. Her father certainly never did. Resolutely she took Holly's hand, and they found their seats and sat low, looking anxiously at the people entering. No Wilkins. Liz breathed a sigh of relief and buckled her seat belt with the casualness of a practiced air traveller. Twenty minutes later everyone was seated. Still no Wilkins. Liz watched with amusement the horror on Holly's face as the stewardess demonstrated the oxygen masks and life vests. 'You wanted to fly, remember,' she teased, 'to experience the twentieth century, to be independent...'

'Right now, I am as independent as Massachusetts in 1620!'

Liz groaned, and with that, the jumbo jet shuddered and began to taxi down the runway.

Holly's wonder at being able to see the lights of towns and cities from such a great height nearly made her forget about Wilkins and the reason they were aboard the giant L-1011—but not for long. Almost as soon as the stewardesses had put away the last of the supper trays, the plane seemed to slow abruptly. A voice filled the cabin: 'Ladies and gentlemen. This is Captain Greene again. We are now ready for our final approach to Moisant International Airport, and I ask that you fasten your seat belts and put your seats in their upright position. Those of you on the left side of the aircraft will be able to see the lights of New Orleans as we turn over Lake Ponchartrain. The weather is clear. The temperature is now at seventy-four degrees. And remember to set your watches one hour earlier. Thank you.'

The L-1011 landed with barely a bump; the great engines roared and helped slow the enormous plane which then turned slowly to taxi toward the arch that marked one end of the main terminal building.

'You see, Holly, we made it,' Liz teased her friend. 'You know, *I* don't understand how these things fly either. I never will. Now let's let Wilkins get off before we do. He must be up there in first class.'

All went well for them; the hotel limousine was waiting outside the baggage-claim area of the airport, and the hotel clerks didn't even question them as they registered at the Hotel Monteleone.

They spent the early evening listening to the Radio Mystery Theatre of the Air which scared Holly more than Liz had expected. It resulted in their discussion of whether ghosts really exist. Liz, of course, reassured Holly.

*T*he girls awoke early to a
sunny, almost tropical day, and dressed quickly.

'Have you ever been to New Orleans, Holly?' Liz asked.

'Of course not,' Holly answered. 'Napoleon had just sold us
the Louisiana Territory at an exorbitant price. It was certainly
not a part of the United States that *I* knew about!'

'Well, you're in for a big surprise, then. Lots has changed
since the days of your Mr Jefferson. It was French then and
mostly woods and Indian towns. . . but it did double our land.'

Since it would be some time before Sean Wilkins's institute
opened, Liz and Holly took a circuitous route from their hotel,
zigzagging through the busy, narrow streets of the Vieux
Carré—the old French Quarter.

'Mom and Dad brought me here once, when we were on our
way to an archaeological meeting in Yucatán,' Liz recalled
soberly as they paused to look in the window of a jewellery store
on Chartres Street. It's just fantastic at night. You wouldn't
believe all the people!'

'Truly,' agreed Holly. 'You know, I would not mind living

in one of these houses with the fancy balconies and all the plants. I have too many choices of times and places,' she added reflectively. 'I guess that I shall never decide for sure.'

'Come on,' interrupted Liz. 'You haven't seen the trolley yet. . .or Saint Charles Avenue. The institute will be opening soon.'

Together they left the French Quarter, over Canal Street, and waited with a small group of people.

'It is like a bus,' Holly exclaimed as the trolley lumbered around the corner and stopped. 'No, more like a train. . .but what are all those ropes?'

'Hush, Holly,' said Liz in mock disgust. 'These are wires. People will think you're from way out in the sticks somewhere!'

'Sticks?'

'Just get on, please.'

The girls sat on a hard but comfortable wooden bench as the trolley slowly made its way down the street, around a big traffic circle, and began the long run out St. Charles Avenue on the inconspicuous tracks that lay on the grass median which separates the busy lanes of cars.

'Watch out for Leontine Street,' Liz said. 'The institute is near there somewhere. Should be fairly easy to spot—it's a new building.'

The street signs came and went—some were those of the Muses: Terpsichore, Clio, and others—but no Leontine. 'Are you sure about the street, Liz?' Holly asked anxiously.

'Pretty sure,' Liz said, beginning to wonder. 'Let's wait a little while longer. I know that if we get to a big park on the left, we've gone too far. That would be about where Tulane University is.'

'There,' Holly said, 'Leontine Street is next.'

Liz pulled the signal cord. The trolley ground to a halt, and the girls jumped onto the grass. They searched both sides of the street carefully, trying to find their destination in what appeared to be a quiet tree-lined residential area.

'There it is, it's got to be,' Liz said. 'About where the trolley is now. We should have gotten off there.'

INSTITUTE FOR CENTRAL AMERICAN RESEARCH, read the

127

small brass plaque beside the glass doors of the white stone building.

'It is not as big as I would have thought,' Holly said as they tried the door. It was open, and they passed into an elegant foyer with dark marble floors and walls that matched the smooth white stone outside. The brass door of an elevator broke the monotony of one wall. The small desk opposite it was empty, but a light shone on one of the buttons of the beige phone.

'*Someone* must be here, then,' Liz reasoned. 'Let's wait a second, then try the elevator. There are only two floors.'

'This looks like the bank we saw in Washington,' Holly said. 'It even has one of those...what did you call them, Liz?...those things,' she continued, pointing up into the corner of the hall.

'Closed circuit TV cameras,' Liz whistled. 'Boy, this sure is fancy!'

Sean Wilkins had arrived very early, buzzed the night guard, and went straight to his upstairs office.

Wilkins hoped to finish a few sensitive overseas phone calls before his secretary arrived. Settling himself behind his mahogany desk, he touched his snarling jade Olmec figurine for luck and dialled the Paris home of one of the institute's most generous patrons.

'Hello, Monsieur Joliet. Did you get... *On a recu mon message?*' Wilkins said smoothly into the receiver. 'Seventy-five thousand dollars... *soixante-quinze*... that's correct. It's worth at least one hundred and seventy-thousand on the open market... *cent soixante-quinze*. There's nothing like it in New York, the USSR, Switzerland, or even Beverly Hills— anywhere... *dans le monde.* Frankly, if you're not interested, I have an Arabian buyer who's willing to pay... *s'il vous plaît, Henri, il ne faut pas parier.* Don't bargain. And most of my other clients get the damn things through customs themselves...'

Startled by a sound in his outer office, Wilkins looked up from the phone and flipped a switch, turning on the closed circuit TV monitor over his desk, just in time to see Liz and

128

Holly as they tiptoed out of the elevator into the hallway.

'Of course, Joliet, *je comprends*,' he said, all the while rotating the camera selection dial to keep the girls on the monitor. *Soyez tranquille*...let's wrap it up quickly...Yes...Yes, it's yours for seventy...*soixante-dix mille.*'

'*Très bien*, Wilkins...*magnifique!*' Wilkins said to himself, adjusting his collar momentarily.

As soon as he put down the phone, his business manner dissolved. Smiling broadly, he sat back to watch the progress of his two uninvited guests.

'Holly, we'd better get out of here. No one's around yet. I told you people don't get to work this early in the morning.'

'The doors were open, were they not?' Holly said as both girls made their way uncertainly back toward the elevator. 'Look, Liz, here is another door!' she cried, quickly pushing her way through a door marked by a red exit sign. Liz ran after her, not noticing the sign on the door: EMERGENCY EXIT ONLY. NO UNAUTHORIZED PERSONNEL. By the time the door slammed shut behind her, Holly was already two flights down shouting something about Icarus.

Liz found her friend standing in what must have been the basement, beside a huge packing crate stencilled with the address: ICARUS, NEW ORLEANS, CHICLE PRODUCTS FOR EXPORT. PRODUCTORES TROPICALES.

'Icarus was the man who tried to fly with homemade wings,' Holly said wistfully. 'I thought that was what flying to New Orleans would be like.'

'Quit kidding around, Holly,' Liz snapped. 'ICARUS stands for Institute for Central American Research, United States Office; it's an acronym, you see. But what I don't understand is why Wilkins needs this much chicle. Either he's the world's biggest chewing-gum freak, or there's some monkey business going on here.'

Monkeys...freaks...acronyms...Confused by twentieth-century language, Holly was momentarily confused.

'We shall just have to march right back up into the reception room, wait for Mr Wilkins to arrive, and ask him straight out about the diaries,' Holly said. 'He doesn't have to know we saw this. Anyway, the worst that can happen is that he will tell us to go away.'

The girls climbed the storeroom steps and crept cautiously into the still-empty foyer as Wilkins followd them on the monitor.

He rose and took the elevator down to where the girls were.

'This is certainly a pleasant surprise,' Wilkins said cordially as he stepped off the elevator. 'When I told you your mother would be welcome in New Orleans, I had no idea that the two of you were planning to come.'

'I hope you do not think we have been forward,' Holly said in her politest manner. 'We just happened to be in town and we thought we would drop by.'

Wilkins invited them into his office. Liz came right to the point. 'Actually we were still curious about my father's diaries. My mother thought it would be nice for me to have copies of everything he ever wrote in case I ever decide to write a book about him. Mum's in publishing, you know, and we thought perhaps you could search the crates of stuff you have in your basement to see if there are any more papers.'

'What makes you think I have "crates of stuff," as you put it, in my basement?'

'Why, you told us so in Washington,' Holly said innocently. 'We would be happy to help you unpack them if you are in need of assistance.'

'That's quite unnecessary, thank you, Miss Holly. I'm afraid all of those crates have been thoroughly examined. There is nothing in them but stones and carvings and pieces of pottery. Very beautiful and valuable, perhaps, but of no significance to anyone except experts in the field.'

'What a pity,' Holly said. 'I had so hoped that there would be some more pictures of that lovely cat. . .what do you call it? 'Oh, yes, the jag-u-ar that Mr Dutton was searching for.'

'I'm afraid you don't understand archaeology very well, Miss Holly. Mel wasn't hunting jaguars, he was an archaeologist, and that's quite a dull job, generally speaking.'

'But when my dad sent me that pendant,' Liz interrupted,

'he did say that it was a picture of something that he was tracking down.'

'Oh, really?' Wilkins perked up. 'What else did he say?'

'Nothing much. Just that he hoped I would have a chance to visit Tikal some day, to see where he had been working. But I suppose that's impossible,' Liz said, feigning disinterest.

'I certainly think it would be impossible for the two of you...Maybe not...But I can see what you have in mind. I can see right through you.'

Holly looked down at herself and replied, 'Oh no, I am definitely opaque.' ·

'How does one travel to Tikal?' Liz asked.

'Normally with scheduled airlines. But if one does not have a passport or proof of U.S. citizenship on hand, one must travel less obviously.'

'Is there no bus transportation?' Holly persisted. 'There seem to be everywhere else we have gone.'

'From Mexico City, you can easily find a guide who will arrange a bus through the Mexican state of Chiapas and then a boat ride up the Usumacinta River into Guatemala.' Wilkins replied.

'U-su-ma-cin-ta? asked Holly, storing the name away in her mind.

'Yes, a very romantic name. It is in the middle of a primitive region far from modern conveniences and communications— exciting for an adult, perhaps, but no place for two young girls alone, believe me. You'd find yourselves in trouble—major trouble—before you knew it.'

'I guess we've come to the end of the trail,' Liz said dejectedly as she repacked the suitcase in the hotel room. 'Wilkins says we can't go to Guatemala by ourselves.'

'I find the manner of that man a trifle suspect. I would be ashamed to think that I let *him* talk me out of doing something I wanted to do. Where's your courage?'

'But, Holly, he's right. It is a long way, and we don't have passports and besides...we *are* just kids.'

'I am not a kid. Remember, I was born in 1790.'

Dejean's Olympia Brass Band led the mourners of an old-time funeral procession down North Rampart Street. At the head strutted two uninhibited grand marshals. One was gaily attired in red tails with a wide, green sash across his chest.

'No offense, Holly, but I don't know what you are. You've been such a good friend that I haven't thought about it much since that night back at Grandma's . . .'

'So, will you heed my advice or the advice of that . . . that Wilkins? I suspect he is the kind of whom Poor Richard said, "The Lying Habit is in some so strong, To Truth they know not how to bend their tongues." '

'You win,' Liz sighed. 'But if we're going, we'd better get out of this hotel. Looks like rain. Besides, I have a feeling Mum and Danny could show up any minute. Let's do some shopping. I think we need some warm weather gear.'

When they went to the desk to turn in the key, Liz reminded the clerk that the room to be held for Mrs Dutton who was arriving momentarily.

Early dusk met the leaden sky. A brief shower subsided almost as quickly as it had begun and left the narrow, wet streets alive with myriad reflections of the lights of New Orleans.

Liz and Holly reached the street outside the hotel and ambled through the French Quarter. Soon they found themselves smack in the middle of a parade. Dejean's Olympia Brass Band led the mourners of an old-time funeral procession down North Rampart Street. At the head strutted two uninhibited grand marshals. One was gaily attired in red tails with a wide, green sash across his chest. In one hand he rhythmically tapped a tambourine against his thigh while held high in the air of the other was a black-fringed red umbrella. The other grand marshal dressed more sombrely for the occasion: black tails, black umbrella, and a black bowler hat held reverently over his heart.

The trumpeter leaned back and pointed his horn at the sky. The first notes of 'When the Saints Go Marching In' pierced the air. The second-liners erupted and pandemonium broke loose—dancing, umbrella-twirling, strutting, stomping, and much hand-clapping. A torrent of jazz swept Liz and Holly along with the hundreds of joyous people.

The band then surged into 'Whoopin' Blues' with the enthusiastic response of the second-liners, a booming yell of

133

'*YEAH!*' The trumpet pealed, hitting higher and higher notes as the music reverberated through the streets.

'Didn't they roll? *YEAH!* Didn't they ramble? *YEAH!*

'Oh, lordy,' gushed an elderly mourner in white satin and jewels, her black skin a beautiful contrast to her white hair and dress. 'Ain't it just nice? Didn't they bury Papa Joe well?' she confided to Holly.

'Yeah, you know it,' said Holly breathlessly. Then, having caught herself slipping out of character, she turned to Liz and said, 'I must confess I rather like your modern hymns.'

Singing and strutting in imitation of the musicians, the crowd made its way up the block, and traffic backed up behind them.

'Used to be just Mardi Gras, now it's every damn day, if you'll excuse the language, ma'am,' muttered the harassed cab driver as his cab stalled out in the heated traffic jam. 'You'd be better off walking to the hotel from here. It's a lot faster.'

Hurriedly Elaine Dutton paid the fare and turned to follow her son toward the hotel.

Liz and Holly were attracted by a nearby clothing store and proceeded to indulge themselves. By now Holly had accepted modern clothing as practical, though the one vestige of the past she would not part with was her sunbonnet.

*B*y five o'clock on Tuesday Elaine Dutton and Danny were seated on the luxurious leather sofa in Sean Wilkins's private office at ICAR.

'You say you haven't seen your daughter since before Thanksgiving?' Wilkins asked Elaine solicitously. 'But what makes you think she would come all the way to New Orleans?'

'I know...'Danny began, but Elaine silenced him with a wave of her hand.

'Danny seems to think that they were headed here. Liz and her friend Holly, that is,' Elaine explained.

'Oh, yes. Holly must be the little girl I saw in Washington. Very charming indeed. She and your daughter seem to be very close friends.'

'You've actually seen Holly, then?'

'Yes, I told you I'd seen them,' Wilkins said with mild annoyance, 'at the Smithsonian with Clive Witherspoon. I assure you, if we'd had any idea that they were runaways, we wouldn't have allowed them to leave. They gave me the impression they were on a school trip of some sort...'

'Thank you, Sean. I'm afraid I've delayed too long in turning this matter over to the police.' Elaine rose to leave, nodding for Danny to follow her.

'Well, do what you think best, Elaine. But perhaps you should give Liz a little more time. She did seem a competent sort, and children nowadays are much more independent than we ever were. Perhaps she just needs to work out her grief in her own way. Please excuse me now. I have some rather pressing business.' He rose suddenly, indicating dismissal, but hesitated, then warmly turned to Elaine as he was nearing the door. 'However, if you're free later, perhaps we could have dinner together. . . and, of course, discuss Liz. It's been much too long since we've sampled some of Antoine's delicious Oysters Rockefeller.'

Her self-control restrained her indignation at Wilkins's flippant suggestion. 'No, thank you. We really must devote all our time to locating Liz. This situation has become entirely out of hand.'

'It certainly has,' Wilkins said to himself as he closed the door behind them. Loosening his sik tie and removing his jacket, he walked over to the bar cabinet that stood next to the small refrigerator. Reaching inside, he took out a bottle of Scotch and poured a stiff drink and then carefully replaced the bottle before running his hand along an inlaid wood panel on the inner floor of the cabinet. The panel swung upward at his touch, and Wilkins extracted a weather-beaten, slightly mouldy, hardbound notebook. Carrying both the drink and his notebook to the sofa, Wilkins settled into its soft leather cushions and prepared to read yet again the diary entry he had kept Mel Dutton from completing. . .

Tikal, Guatemala   March 27

 The clues to the location of the lost
Jaguar City are coming together now, and
the focus is Temple IV, where the butt of
the stela may still be in place. I am
now convinced that a seventh-century
ruler — certainly one of the Jaguar family
lineage — left Tikal to found a new
city, perhaps just before October 28, 627,
and before Temple IV was built.

 The new fragment dates _after_ the
construction of Temple IV and marks the
anniversary of the old event. Therefore,
we know that whatever happened, it
was very important and had been for
a long time. God, it's so Maya, this
system of dates and anniversaries. I
believe that this pyramid is somehow
pointing to the Jaguar City. But
which way? Can I, now, possibly pick

up on this very cold trail of clues?

I should probably return to the
States to consult my old friend, Herschel
Goodman. But I have practical reasons
for not wanting to leave the Petén. I
am increasingly uneasy about my
relationship with Sean Wilkins. Art
detective that he may be, the roles of
cops and robbers are often inter-
changeable. I am unhappy about his
absurd obsession with Cortés's gold,
his incessant trips back and forth
to New Orleans, his lack of patience
with the crews

The diary broke off in mid-sentence. That must have been where Mel Dutton interrupted his writing and snuffed out his kerosene lamp to check the sound of the truck approaching his tent from the direction of the main excavation headquarters, Sean Wilkins thought. Dutton had followed that truck on foot the short distance to the airstrip where it met Wilkins's DC-3 and had seen two men hastily unloading a large crate.

Sean Wilkins remembered bitterly every word of the encounter that followed...

'Wilkins, didn't expect to see you back in camp so soon,' Mel Dutton said, stepping from the night-shrouded jungle into the glare of the truck's headlights. 'Night landings are rather dangerous under these conditions, though I see you did have someone set up a few flares for you.'

'Good to see you, old man,' he answered Dutton, more discomforted than pleased. 'You're right. I don't particularly fancy landing at this time, but we had bad conditions getting out of New Orleans, and I didn't feel like waiting until tomorrow. Weather reports said it might storm again and then God knows when I'd get these supplies in here...'

'You appear to be loading supplies, not unloading them,' Dutton replied, stepping over to examine the crate that the two porters had deposited near the plane. 'Chicle... Wilkins, we're not in the chewing-gum business here. What the hell is going on?'

'Simply a way of avoiding red tape...' Wilkins began with a laugh. 'As you can see, everything is in order—they are marked for delivery to ICAR...'

'In order. What do you mean "in order"? We made no arrangements to ship anything out to ICAR or anywhere else. You know damn well that nothing is supposed to leave Guatemala unless it has been catalogued and okayed for temporary loan by the institute. You're a smuggler and a looter, Wilkins!'

'I prefer to think of myself as an art lover,' Wilkins said calmly. 'The notion that all of these beautiful, priceless objects should remain here in this stupid backwater country is nothing but shortsighted nationalist propaganda. Don't you see that? What if they were destroyed during a revolution or some natural disaster? I save them from oblivion and place these treasures in the hands of legitimate collectors who can appreciate and

139

care for them much better than some second-rate local curator possibly could.'

'You're robbing these people of their artistic heritage, and you're using me to do it.'

'Using you? Dutton, I'm giving you the chance of a lifetime. I'm not greedy. All I want are a few stelae, a few polychrome vases—a fraction of what's buried here... and maybe a shot at some gold. And, in exchange, I'm making it possible for you to go on with your work, find your little finds, photograph, calculate, gaze at the stars, work on your mysterious puzzles... and maybe even find the lost Jaguar city which I've been reading about in your notes...'

'My notes? You've been...'

'May I remind you that your alternatives are few. I'm not an amateur at this game, you know. I have an organization. I "own" quite a few important people, and even if you did manage to get someone who was interested in listening to your charges against me, do you think they'd take your word for it? I've been careful to mention your name in the course of my little transactions... your signature has been forged on ICAR's records. By the time we straightened out the question of which one of us is indeed the looter, my private staff here in Petén may well have located your precious city. You don't suppose you're the only one searching for the Jaguar city, do you? I've got chicleros combing the jungle for it right this minute... and if they find it, they'll know exactly how to preserve its precious stones, even if I'm not there to direct them.'

'I'm not going to let you get away with this, Wilkins. I'll be damned if I cooperate with someone who stands for everything I've been fighting all these years.'

'Think it over, Dutton. You can come out of this jungle a famous scientist and a rich man, or you can run the risk of not coming out at all. I'll give you until tomorrow to answer...'

'Of course, I didn't give him until morning,' Wilkins mumbled from the depths of his office sofa. He remembered how that very night he had sent Raúl, his most trusted *chiclero*, to Dutton's camp. Not an hour later Raúl had come back and described how he had plunged his machete through the tent, slicing through Dutton's abdomen. 'Dutton never made a sound,' he had said, and he had embellished the story further as

140

he spoke of the feel of the machete blade as it sliced through the man. The next day he showed Wilkins the evidence...the ripped tent, blood all over the cot, Dutton's diary still lying there on the stool where he must have placed it before going to sleep.

But then those damned rumours had started. Three months after Raúl 'killed' Dutton, Wilkins began hearing that there was a white man travelling in the jungle. He thought they were just stories, legends made up by the locals—until he heard the man described as tall, heavily bearded, and auburn haired.

He had had no choice then but to eliminate Raúl Uc. He had made his assistant, Emiliano Guzmán, help him. With a sneer he recalled how he had sent the Indian ahead of them down into the dark void of the abandoned tomb chamber near Temple IV, then the blow on the head, and the sealing of the opening with the big limestone slab. Raúl could not have survived *that*.

Sean Wilkins closed Dutton's diary, running the tips of his long slender fingers over the bloodstained binding. 'Animal blood,' he said aloud. 'And now two snippy kids asking half the archaeologists on the East Coast leading questions about jaguars and lost cities...'

Sean Wilkins was a fussy man. He liked his plans neat and tidy, and when they weren't, he began to get very nervous indeed. He poured himself another Scotch.

*T*he cross-section of people milling about the terminal of Moisant Airport in New Orleans included old couples in cowboy attire on vacation, young skiers, and several young men in their late twenties, conservatively dressed and wearing dark glasses.

'This is crazy,' Liz whispered to Holly as they sat in the huge waiting room. 'It says right here in plain English that to leave the United States for Mexico, you must either have a valid passport or a tourist card. And that rotten Wilkins told us we could get in through Mexico.'

'We evidently do need some aid,' Holly said.

'Listen, Holly, it also says that "tourist cards are not issued without proof of citizenship." Period. No exceptions. And also, we're minors.'

'I thought a miner was someone who digs in the ground for gold or coal or...'

'Y'sure are one crazy bird. Like your threads too,' came a voice from a tall young man behind them. Liz wheeled around and stared at the four young men who sat nearby. All four were dressed in expensive-looking three-piece business suits with light blue dress shirts and were carrying briefcases and copies of *The Wall Street Journal*. It seemed impossible that the voice she had heard belonged to any one of this group.

'Ow! Don' eye us like that, it 'urts, man,' one of the 'businessmen' wailed. 'Y'think we like these bleedin' getups any better'n you do?'

'They must be seafaring men,' Holly whispered to Liz. 'One of them has an earring.'

'I'm Freddie,' said the man. 'Lead guitar. This 'ere's George Rigby, on bass. Over 'ere, 'Arvey Willis, drums. Orv Simpson there does a bit o' sax.'

'My name's Elizabeth Dutton,' said Liz. 'And this is my friend Holly Hobbie.'

'Couldn't 'elp over'ear you two 'bout not 'avin' a tourist card'n all. Maybe we can 'elp.'

At that moment the four young men were joined by a fifth, who was staggering under an impossible load of tote bags, music cases, and cameras. ''Erman, y'made it,' said Freddie. Turning to the girls he said, 'This is 'Erman, our roadie—our manager.' Then, pulling the overburdened newcomer off to one side, he began whispering furiously and pointing in Liz and Holly's direction. Herman stared at them dubiously.

''Oo are these two?' Herman said.

'This 'ere is Liz Dutton and 'er friend, one 'Olly 'Obbie,' Freddie said.

'Well, there certainly would not be *two* of me,' Holly snapped back.

'Awl right, awl right,' he wailed as at last a voice over the loudspeaker announced the departure for Mexico City. The young men stood up to board the plane, and Herman motioned for the girls to join them. 'You birds stick like glue,' he whispered conspiratorially, and a minute later he casually fanned out a thick handful of passports in his palm and the whole group passed through security without incident. Astonishingly they ended up on the plane. Fortunately it was not full.

By takeoff time Liz, Holly, and their new companions had settled into the first-class compartment, and the four young

143

men were busily stripping off their jackets and shirts to reveal a wild assortment of death's-head T-shirts, chain-link jewellery, and wicked-looking tattoos. Holly was now sure that they had fallen into the hands of a band of modern-day pirates. Then the young man with the earring grabbed a music case from Herman and produced a guitar. 'This is terrif, positively terrif,' Herman crowed. 'Punk rock 'eads south of the border! I bet the Mexicans ain't never seen the like o' us!'

Harvey began pounding out the percolating percussion of a crude bongo-drum beat, and the whole group broke into a hard-driving rendition of a sound barely recognizable as 'South of the Border.' Liz jumped up and began dancing in the aisle as an ashen-faced stewardess looked on helplessly.

Holly watched with apprehension for a few seconds, but seeing that the stewardess seemed to have accepted the mayhem, decided that she might as well join in and enjoy herself.

''Ow old are you guls, anyway?' Herman shouted to Holly over the din.

'She's thirteen, and I'm one hundred eighty-nine,' Holly answered mischievously.

'Far out, man, far out,' Herman exclaimed as he popped open one of the locked briefcases, pulled out a hard-boiled egg and a leg of Kentucky Fried Chicken, and settled down to a quick snack.

The sudden departure from New Orleans of the punk rock group 'Umble Grites, after a concert where they started a riot by pelting their fans with eggs and rotten tomatoes, made the lead story on local TV that evening. Two of the major networks picked up the story for their news broadcasts, but ABC, guessing that punk rock mayhem was already passé, decided instead to feature a live interview conducted by their popular New Orleans correspondent, Lucy LaBelle. As Lucy LaBelle promised, the story had plenty of human interest: a thirteen-year-old searching vainly for her world-renowned archaeologist father; the mystery girl, Holly Hobbie; even the sophisticated New York editor, Elaine Dutton, baring her heart as she talked about her grief for her famous husband.

'Mel loves life, and he loves the Maya people,' Elaine told the nationwide audience. 'He was never happier than when he was tracking down some mysterious temple, and he believes deeply that by uncovering the secrets of the ancient Maya, he contributes to the betterment of mankind... We have never given up hope of finding him alive, and I believe that my daughter, Liz, before she disappeared, discovered some new evidence that might lead us to him...Now she, too, is lost, and my son, Daniel...'

Elaine turned and looked around for Danny who was kneeling below the camera view. 'Danny, sit up!' Elaine whispered out of the side of her mouth.

'I couldn't find my microphone, Mum!' Danny said, as he sat back up in his chair next to Elaine and adjusted his lapel microphone.

'...and we appeal to anyone who might have seen her and her friend to contact this station immediately.'

'Just last summer,' Lucy LaBelle explained to the viewers, 'Elaine Dutton was in Guatemala, leading the search for her husband, Melville, who was reported missing in early May. According to Dutton's partner, New Orleans archaeologist and antiquarian, Sean Wilkins, Melville Dutton had been depressed over his failure to decipher some hieroglyphics he had been studying for the past year and had announced that he was planning to spend two months incommunicado, working at a secret jungle camp he had established. Teams of helicopters crisscrossed the dense jungles, finding no trace of the missing professor.

'Now Elaine Dutton faces yet another tragedy. Her thirteen-year-old daughter has disappeared. We have reason to believe that she was in the New Orleans vicinity. The pictures you are now seeing on your TV screens are a recent photo of thirteen-year-old Liz Dutton and an artist's rendition of the mysterious companion, identified only as Holly, who is believed to be travelling with her. Anyone who has any information about either of these girls, please call this special toll-free number: 800-555-1200.

'This is Lucy LaBelle, WVUE in New Orleans. And

now back to Barbara Walters in New York.'

Even Hal Abbot, who had watched Lucy LaBelle's interview on television, was impressed with Elaine's performance. 'That was a nice touch,' he told her when he called her hotel room. 'That bit about never giving up hope of finding Mel alive. But you don't really mean it, I hope. A smart girl like you must realize that Mel Dutton isn't going to come walking out of that jungle after nine months without a word. Besides, your long-distance husband seems to have been getting away from you *before* he disappeared. What kind of a man would plan to spend two months in the jungle without even sending a letter to his wife? Your husband was a fanatic. . .'

'By your definition, Hal, perhaps he *is*. Liz is a fanatic too, for that matter, and her faith has made me remember why I fell in love with Mel in the first place. Maybe Mel wasn't always around, maybe he left the practical problems of raising a family to me, but when we were together, life was exciting. How many women get to explore the Amazon on their honeymoon? How many have an archaeological site in Mexico named after them? I saw it when we went down for the search. Mel discovered it and as it had no recorded name, he called it 'Elena de las Flores'—Elaine of the Flowers. . .'

'Elena de las Flores,' Hal said sorrowfully. 'If you ever decide to give up these romantic notions and grow up, let me know. Meanwhile I seem to remember that you left a publishing company back here.'

Danny Dutton looked at his mother's face as she was hanging up. 'Forget about that creep,' Danny said, taking his mother's arm. 'We don't need Hal. Besides, he better get it in gear.'

Freddie, sixteen and the youngest member of the band, was rapidly developing a crush on Holly. Nothing could have suited their purposes better, Liz decided, for Freddie took it upon himself to argue their case with Herman, who was beginning to have last minute doubts about the wisdom of arriving in Mexico City in the company of two underage and unidentified girls. Still Liz was surprised to feel a twinge of jealousy as she watched Holly and Freddie laughing over their in-flight dinners.

No point in being jealous of a girl who's almost two hundred years old, Liz tried to convince herself as she took a seat beside Herman for her own meal. Here she was, flying unchaperoned for the second time in two days, having slipped over the border thanks to a band of famous rock stars—well, almost famous rock stars. The girls back in school would be green with envy, but all she could think about was why Freddie was attracted to Holly instead of her. Holly was so...so childish.

Liz took a healthy bite of her steak and, as if to demonstrate her own maturity, took a sip of the champagne Herman offered her. It tasted strange, not at all like the sweet wines Grandma Dutton sometimes served at Sturbridge. Liz took another determined swallow and hoped no one would notice the face she made. It was unlikely that anyone would. George, Harvey, and Orv were deep in a discussion of some new bit they had planned for their Mexico City appearance. Liz studied the backs of their heads for a minute or so and decided that they were all pretty old—in their twenties, at least. Only Freddie was really young enough to be interested, and he and Holly clearly didn't need any company.

'It's 'er accent,' Herman said confidentially.

'What?' Liz asked dumbly, embarrassed to realize that Herman had been watching her stare at Holly.

''Er accent. 'Er bloody way a speakin'. Freddie loves 'igh-class English guls, and he figures your friend is one of 'em. Wants to learn to speak like an English chap, 'e does. I tell 'im I'm English. Talk like me. But 'e won't 've none o' it.'

'Excuse me, but isn't Freddie English? I thought you were all from the East End of London.'

'Naw...' Herman seemed vastly amused. 'Freddie's from Alabama originally. 'E was livin' in 'Ollywood when we 'ired 'im after our first drummer, Ron, left us for a gig with the 'Ari Krishnas.'

'I never heard of a rock group by that name,' Liz said, puzzled.

'Ain't a rock group. Buncha bald chaps 'oo raise veggies and sell incense and all.'

Liz began to feel that the conversation was getting away from her. 'But isn't any of it real? Can you just be a punk rocker one day and a Hare Krishna the next?'

'People change,' Herman shrugged cheerfully and motioned for the stewardess. 'Couple a Cokes over 'ere, if ya don' mind. We're too young ta be drownin' our livers in this bubbly.'

Liz blanched, half expecting the stewardess to become suspicious now that Herman had drawn attention to her age.

'See,' said Herman reassuringly, as two large Cokes with ice were delivered without comment. 'She don' care 'ow old ya are. No one cares...long as ya ain't runnin' away from 'ome on yer mum's credit cards.'

Herman's guess was too close for comfort.

'It's true that we have my mother's credit cards,' Liz protested. 'But we're not running away...'

Before she realized what she was doing, Liz found herself telling Herman the whole story. He listened intently, nodding his head as if lost cities, mysterious disappearances, and girls who step out of picture frames were everyday occurrences. It was Liz, going over the events of the past few days in her own mind, who found her situation unbelievable.

'...so here we are,' she concluded, 'arriving in Mexico City in a few minutes, and I have no idea how we're going to get to Guatemala, much less find my father. I can't even remember how to ask the way in Spanish. When I'm with Holly, she always makes me feel that anything is possible. She's so sure of herself. I wish I were.'

Herman sniffed. 'You're the one 'oo's sure your old man's still alive, ain't cha? You're the one 'oo figured out 'ow to get this far. So maybe you got some special powers 'elpin' ya out.'

Herman looked thoughtful. 'You're just worried about wot folks'll say or wot'll 'appen if ya end up 'avin' to call yer mum to come getcha like a little kid.'

'I guess so. It would be humiliating...like the time I thought I was really smart and wrote across my history final, ''Only God knows these answers!'' When I got back my exam,

148

the teacher had written, "God gets an A, you get an F!" '

'So the worst that can 'appen is your act will get a bad review. 'Appens to everyone.' Herman smiled shyly. 'For the record, I give yer act an A plus.'

Before Liz had time to thank him properly for his consolation, the screen had dropped into place for the in-flight movie. Liz paid the stewardess for two sets of earphones, put hers on, and asked the stewardess to hand the other to Holly. When Holly tore herself away from Freddie long enough to look up at the headpiece being offered to her, Liz called, 'It's the movie *Jaws*, Holly! Put on the earphones!'

Holly didn't understand, but put them on anyway. A couple of days before she had learned what a phone was for the first time, but that one had a mouthpiece as well as an earpiece on it. Now Holly tried to position the earphone so one earpiece went on her mouth and the other on an ear, but she corrected herself when she saw how Liz was wearing them. She wondered for a moment whether twentieth-century folk could talk with their ears.

'Put the dial on two, Holly!' Liz called. She was happy to keep Holly's attention away from Freddie for a minute. Holly put the dial on two. 'Now watch the screen!' said Liz.

Suddenly the terrifying face of a shark appeared, racing forward on the screen and growing more colossal each moment till its teeth were long, gnashing spears directly before Holly's eyes. At the same time horrifying screams reverberated in Holly's head. She threw her hands in front of her face, then flung off the earphones and jumped up to escape the attack. As she started up the aisle, her head blocked the screen and several voices chimed in, 'Down in front! Down in front!' Thinking that they meant the shark was in the extreme front of the plane, exactly where she was heading, Holly backed into a corner by the emergency exit and was about to try to get the door open when Liz reached her to calm her down and explain in a soothing voice what a movie was. 'Also, Holly,' she finished, 'if you go out that door you'll be falling for the next hour.'

By the time the plane began its descent over Mexico City,

Liz felt that Herman wasn't such a weird guy after all. He was much too old for her, of course, probably even older than the rest of the group...but...

Wondering just where their conversation might have led if they hadn't been interrupted kept Liz occupied for the last few minutes of the flight. She had no time at all to worry about what would happen when she and Holly tried to bluff their way past the Mexican immigration authorities.

Unknown to its passengers Eastern flight 907 from New Orleans was landing at an airport that was virtually an armed camp. Mexico City had been stirring for days with rumours of the impending arrival of a British punk rock group. Denouncing the whole phenomenon as decadent, the conservative newspapers had refused to advertise the concert; nevertheless word of the group's travel plans had gone out over the grapevine and a substantial crowd of teenagers, more curious than admiring, had converged on the airport.

The crowd was very distressing to airport police—probably the ony group in town to be fooled by the news blackout. Mistaking the activity for the beginnings of a political demonstration, they ordered reinforcements from downtown and isolated the crowd behind barriers in the lounge, waiting for the main body of demonstrators to appear with signs and slogans. By the time word filtered up to Police Captain Gómez informing him of the real reason for the commotion, New Orleans passengers were already leaving the plane.

Captain Gómez acted quickly, ordering his men to refuse entry to the troublemakers. But the band had changed back into their 'straight' clothes, and Gómez's men seized on a group of bearded Canadian backpackers who were totally bewildered to find themselves surrounded by immigration police accusing them in thick Spanish accents of being ''Umble Grites,' while behind barricades a crowd of several hundred shouted encouragement and hooted at the police.

Meanwhile a harried Herman managed to hustle Liz, Holly, and the musicians, now conservatively dressed, and eighteen pieces of luggage passed customs and into two waiting cabs. No one paid them the slightest bit of attention.

No one, that is, except young Jaime Rojas, who had been assigned to meed the plane and pick up two young girls travelling alone. Seeing Liz and Holly surrounded by five conservatively dressed young men, Jaime retreated in confusion. Were they police, FBI men, agents of the competiton, or what? Cursing his luck, Jaime hailed a cab and ordered it to follow the group at a discreet distance. Jaime had no idea what to expect, but when the cabs delivered their passengers in the Zona Rosa, at one of the city's most expensive restaurants, he threw up his hands in despair. He could not afford to follow them inside. He would have to stay in the parking lot all evening.

Inside the restaurant Herman was enthusiastically ordering his second dinner of the evening and urging the others to do the same. Holly was the first to agree, and Liz realized with some chagrin that her worries about Holly adjusting to exotic Mexico had been for nothing. If anything, Holly seemed to feel more at home here than Liz herself did. The language barrier didn't bother her as much as it did Liz, since by now she was used to dealing with a communication gap. And at dinner she surprised everyone by biting happily into a hot chili pepper and announcing that it was almost like the ones her grandfather raised in his garden in Sturbridge. The only thing that seemed to bother Holly about Mexico and Mexican food were the sliced tomatoes that were served with their taco dinners. 'Love apples,' Holly called them, and she was convinced that they were poisonous. When Herman and the musicians insisted on eating them anyway, Holly stared gravely all through dessert, as though expecting them all to collapse in agony any minute. It nearly spoiled everyone's fun until Herman, in a burst of exasperation wailed, 'Cripes, 'Olly, ya look like ya 'spect ta see a ghost!' Much to Herman's surprise, the remark touched off a flurry of giggles from both girls that lasted most of the evening.

'Ladies,' said Herman as the festivities began to wind down. 'We're gonna sack out at the Geneve 'otel down the street. It's a great place, 'cept they don't take credit cards. But the El Presidente does and it's only a block or so away.'

'Holly and I saw it from the taxi as we came in,' Liz said.

This had been an evening neither one would forget.

151

Wednesday, November 29

W

ednesday morning belonged
to Liz and Holly alone, for Herman and the group had to check
to make sure all their sound equipment had arrived and see
that it was set up right. Herman had told Holly that they might
even rehearse.

Liz and Holly wandered the Zona Rosa, the main area of
tourist shops that lay between the teeming avenue of the
Reforma and the crowded circular plaza of the Insurgentes
metro station. As they ambled past store windows filled with
woven shawls and brightly embroidered dresses, Holly's keen
eye for needlework served them well. Within an hour or so both
girls had acquired patterned headbands and shawls. By noon
they were not only tired, but hungry, and sat in the booth of a
short-order restaurant at Insurgentes Circle. The purpose of
their trip loomed again, and Liz began to get nervous about
their travel arrangements.

'Why do we not ask Erman for help,' Holly suggested
between bites of her *quesadilla,* a sort of grilled-cheese turnover
made with a crisp tortilla. 'We certainly know him well enough

now, and he seems to know all about everything.

'*Her*man,' Liz corrected. 'No, I'm afraid Herman has other things to worry about. He's not even sure that Mexico is ready for punk rock,' she remembered with a smile. ''Umble Grites is thinking of changing its image.'

'An interesting concept,' Holly said, 'but, that does not advance our goal.'

'I can't believe we're this far already,' Liz said. 'It's been less than a week since we left Sturbridge—less than a week since you arrived or whatever you call it.'

'I appeared,' Holly corrected with a quiet smile. 'But I have an idea, Liz. Let us do what we did elsewhere: go to the anthropology museum. There may be someone there who can give us good advice.'

Liz paid their small bill, and the girls walked back outside.

'Liz,' Holly said, stopping and pointing. 'There is Maya writing right here.'

Liz looked. The great curving walls of concrete that bracketed the metro entrances were covered from top to bottom with the distinctive symbols that the girls had come to know so well.

'My gosh, Holly,' said Liz ruefully, 'we can't seem to get away from the things, can we.'

'It is an omen,' answered Holly. 'For sure.'

Chapultepec Park seemed like a modern-day Brueghel painting brought to life. Couples strolled beneath the great pines that lined the Paseo de la Reforma; children clambered on the rocky wooded knoll overlooking a small lake filled with boaters and ducks; and picnickers enjoyed their early afternoon meals along the edges of the trees. In the great clearings of foot-worn grass at least a dozen soccer games were in noisy progress. The girls' taxi—a bright yellow Volkswagen with one front seat removed to allow space for the meter—pulled off the Reforma to deposit Liz and Holly in a small area of trees beside a monolith, a great effigy of stone that brooded over the festive atmosphere. Its pedestal bore the sign, MUSEO NACIONAL DE ANTROPOLOGÍA.

Liz and Holly joined the general flow of the big milling

153

crowd, refused the entreaties from four separate vendors who offered guide books and postcards, crossed a wide flagstone plaza, and entered the glass doors that broke the grey stone of the front of the huge building.

The girls checked their parcels near the museum shop and, while Holly browsed among the books, the replicas of pottery figurines, and the large rubbings that hung near the glass cases of gold jewellery, Liz went into the hallway beyond, towards the sign that said, simply, DIRECTOR—the office of the director.

'Pardon me, ma'am, she said hesitantly to a smiling woman behind a desk in the hall. 'Is there an archaeologist here—a Maya archaeologist that I could see?'

'*Lo siento,* I am sorry, señorita,' she replied, 'but the only one would be the director himself, Dr Ruz, and he, unfortunately, is not here. You might try the *instituto* offices on Córdoba Street, but I'm sure that most all the archaeologists would be in the field by now. You see,' she smiled sympathetically, 'this is the dry season—practically their only chance to work in the lowlands.'

'I see,' Liz replied dejectedly. 'Thank you anyway. *Muchas gracias.*' She smiled suddenly, pleased with her new Spanish.

'What a *bummer,*' Holly added in *her* new vernacular when Liz told her the news. 'But we shall not give up. We cannot, Liz. You felt despondent in New Orleans too...remember? And look where we are now. Let us see some of the museum.'

'My mother will never believe how many museums I've been to lately!' Liz said.

Entering the large enclosed patio, the girls were impressed by the great fountain column that supported the graceful square of concrete that seemed to float far above, sheltering the entire patio. As they crossed the open space, a fine spray from the falling water, whipped by a sudden breeze, enveloped them briefly.

'Here,' said Holly, stopping before an open glass door. ' "*La Sala Maya*"—the Maya Hall.'

Just inside, a huge map covered the wall. Liz paused and took in the shape of the Yucatán peninsula and its base.

154

'Holly,' she pointed, stepping forward and indicating the approximate centre of the huge expanse of green. 'This is where we are going. Our only problem now is how to get there. This is the Usumacinta River that Wilkins told us about.' Her finger traced a thin line of blue that led downward to Yaxchilán, then beyond, 'I wonder what it's like there.'

A half hour later the girls decided they were tired and had had their fill of carvings, pots, and sculpture. Outside another door that led from the hall, however, they forgot their weariness, for there in the yard of the museum, between the huge building and the fence along the Reforma, were two exact replicas of Maya temples.

'Gosh,' Liz exclaimed, 'I've seen picture after picture of these things, but I never realized...'

'How magnificent they were,' Holly finished. 'What these must look like in a real jungle!' she exclaimed as she stepped inside and, with Liz at her shoulder, surveyed the bright murals of yard-high figures that covered the walls inside.

'No wonder Dad loved this stuff so,' said Liz thoughtfully. 'Mr Witherspoon was right. Maya things get into your blood. Holly, let's go rest now. My feet are falling off.'

The girls retraced their steps, passed the fountain and the museum shop, retrieved the packages they had checked, and walked out the main entrance. Soon they found an empty bench under a tall pine.

Almost as soon as they had settled down, a clean-cut Mexican man, wearing a grey suit and tie despite the warmish weather, sat down near them. Even if the girls had searched their memories thoroughly, it is doubtful that they would have remembered Jaime Rojas, who had watched them leave the airport with Herman and the rock group.

'You need a guide, senoritas?' asked Jaime hesitantly. 'I can give you a very good tour of the museum and explain the things for you.'

'No thank you,' said Liz. 'We've done enough museum walking for a whole month.'

'What beautiful headbands,' Jaime persisted, still trying to keep the conversation alive. 'But, of course, the weaving here is *nada*, nothing, compared to that of Guatemala.' Jaime had chosen his words skilfully.

'How does one get to Guatemala from here?' Holly ventured casually.

'Ah. señoritas, *es muy fácil,* very easy, if you have the proper papers. You need only to buy the tickets.'

'Suppose one does *not* have the papers—not even a passport or a letter of permission to travel alone?' ventured Liz.

'Then,' Jaime said, grinning broadly, 'it is more difficult, but quite possible. The best arrangement is by way of the Usumacinta River. My uncle happens to be in the business—the travel business, that is. Here's his card. My name is Jaime Rojas. If you should ever need his services, merely go to that address. He is there all the time—except for later this week. He leaves on a trip of his own tomorrow but will only be gone a week or so.'

Liz inspected the small white card. *'Manuel Rojas,'* it read. *'Agencia de Viajes. Versailles No 19.'*

Jaime stood suddenly. 'I must leave now. *Adiós,* señoritas. Remember what I have told you.' He turned and walked away rapidly without looking back.

Liz could not shake her suspicions. How had Guatemala entered the conversation anyway? Could he have overheard them talking about their problem? Still the business card seemed legitimate.

'You know, Liz,' Holly said, 'we could talk to this Manuel Rojas. We do not *have* to go this way if we decide against it later, but now it seems a reasonable choice.'

'About our only choice at the moment,' Liz said. Both girls rose at once and went to one of the taxis parked near the big museum statue.

'This is the address on the card,' Liz said, looking around. The taxi had left them on a corner near a theatre advertising a movie of the Rolling Stones concert. Already a line of perhaps a hundred stood waiting and laughing. Most of them, boys about Liz's age, were dressed in leather jackets, and a few noticed the girls and yelled something.

Holly smiled back. 'I hope this movie does not reduce the number of people that will hear 'Umble Grites tonight,' she said to Liz.

'It's *Humble Greats,*' said Liz resignedly. 'And here's number nineteen.'

The tiny office lay between the theatre and what appeared to be an apartment house. A faded poster, taped inside the dingy plate glass, advertised Acapulco. Yellowed credit-card stickers plastered the translucent glass of the peeling wooden door.

They entered. Manuel Rojas sat apparently dozing in a chair, alongside a bottle of tequila. He was heavily bearded, moustached, with jowls sweating. Slowly he opened an eye and looked upwards. Above him a ceiling fan slowly stirred the air. His hand snapped forward quickly as he caught a fly in midair, crushing it.

'Señoritas, excuse our humble surroundings,' the stoutish man said, rising from behind a large desk covered with glass. His thick moustache rose at the ends as he smiled. 'Our business is small by *norteamericano* standards, but we are very, very good at it. How may I help you?' He motioned to two straight chairs with torn wicker seats.

'We wish to go to Guatemala,' Holly began, 'but we have a slight problem...'

'Ah, you must be the girls my nephew spoke of,' laughed Manuel Rojas—a little *too* heartily, Liz thought. 'Indeed he telephoned me not five minutes ago. And I, of course, am the uncle, Manuel Rojas, *su servidor,* your servant.'

Both girls looked sufficiently impressed, and Rojas continued. 'You have no papers, is that correct? No matter, for anything is possible. For the proper amount of money—five thousand pesos—I will guarantee that you will get where you wish.'

'That's what? About three hundred dollars?' Liz asked, suddenly in a panic. 'Do you take any credit cards?'

'But, of course,' the man assured her. '*All* kinds.' He reached under a pile of newspapers and found the small card-stamping machine.

157

'Then we wish to go,' said Holly. Liz nodded reluctantly in agreement.

'Very well. It is settled. You will meet me tonight at the main bus station—any taxi driver can find it—at precisely eight-thirty. Where are you staying?' Liz named the hotel.

'*Muy bien,* very well,' said the man, satisfied. 'But leave there around eight or, better, a little before. There is some crazy music group in the city tonight—a concert—and traffic may be even worse than usual. You and I will take the bus—I by coincidence am going that way, too, as Jaime may have mentioned. From here we go to Villahermosa, Tabasco, and then to Tenosique town. That is on the river. After that we will see. I will make the arrangements that will put you into Guatemala quickly.'

'It sounds very good to us,' Holly answered. 'We will see you later.'

'Very well, then, señoritas—*hasta luego.* If you will just sign here, please,' Manuel Rojas added, placing the credit-card form in front of Liz.

Holly and Liz strolled through the town. The food markets were closing. Mainly clothes and items of jewellery were being sold. Vendors eager to make sales before the tourists left offered dresses, shawls, and other clothing at reduced prices. Liz and Holly spiced their weary wait by buying some Mexican clothing for the next leg of their journey.

Holly and Liz watched the happy townspeople celebrate a fiesta. They even wrapped themselves, shoulder to ankle, in bright blankets. The Mexican band played and the people danced.

T

ravelling through the night, their bus carried them across the great plateau of central Mexico, first over superhighways, then down winding mountain roads into the steaming coastal plain of the state of Veracruz. They were coming into more and more primitive country. Except for an occasional large town, the cities dwindled to villages, then the villages dwindled to small, single homes, and finally even the isolated homes began to disappear.

Soon they entered the Tuxtla Mountains and the road began to curve more and more as it wound among the old volcanic peaks.

Behind them the sky suddenly seemed to be on fire. Great billows of smoke emanating from the volcano filled the air. Holly looked around frantically. When a particularly dense cloud climbed into the air, Liz and Holly became even more uncomfortable. Manuel, however, remained unperturbed. There was an ominous silence between the girls that seemed to say they were very small here and that the land was very powerful and could have its way with them.

Suddenly there was an explosion! Heads craned back towards the volcanic peak that towered above the road. Holly and Liz clutched at each other. '¡Reventión! ¡Una llanta pinchada! Flat tyre!' called the driver, and Holly and Liz looked at each other with thin smiles. When they relaxed enough to look around, they saw that nobody else had been too worried. The other passengers were talking or sleeping as they had been. Accidents and scares were apparently a natural part of their lives.

Breathing a sigh of relief, Liz looked out the window to see which tyre was flat. Instantly her heart seemed to stick in her throat. The bus had come to rest no more than two inches from the edge of the cliff, and below Liz's eyes was nothing but thousands of feet of space. The blowout had fortunately occurred on the inside part of the road. The driver and his assistant were outside the bus already, whistling merrily as they changed the tyre.

Late Thursday morning the bus made a breakfast stop at Coåtzacoalcos, and had crossed into the Tabasco State. A few hours later Liz, Holly, Manuel, and a handful of the other passengers transferred to a local bus in Chiapas, an eternity, it seemed, beyond Villahermosa. Here the sight of peasant women with marketing baskets and women selling fruits and vegetables waving to them helped the girls to forget their uneasiness. Holly struck up a conversation of sorts with a woman passenger across the aisle, gamely trying to pronounce the Spanish names of everything they passed on the road. And when three roosters escaped from a bamboo cage carried by one old man passenger, Liz joined in the good-natured mayhem until they were recaptured.

Manuel had asked the bus driver to let them off at an inconspicuous crossroads a few miles beyond the centre of Tenosique.

'I am as stiff from sitting as if I were back in my portrait,' Holly said. 'Is there time for a few bends and stretches?'

The travel agent turned around and smiled at them both. 'You shall be able to rest soon,' he said.

Then they were met by a Maya whom Manuel called Chan. After spending Thursday night with Chan's family, Manuel explained, they would fly south early Friday morning.

'We must fly early in the mornings here. There are too many thunderstorms later in the day.'

Chan's home turned out to be a two-room thatch-roofed hut which he shared with his wife, Amelia, and four small children. As far as Liz could tell, Amelia understood only the language of the Maya. Chan, though he appeared to understand Spanish when Manuel spoke to him, seldom uttered a sound in any language. And Manuel did not seem interested in making conversation. The girls looked at each other as though to ask, 'What next?'

After they shared the family's meal of black beans and tortillas, Amelia produced a spare hammock which she hung in the room the family normally used as a kitchen and eating area. Pantomiming shyly, she showed Liz and Holly that this was to be their bed for the night. Liz had seen these fragile-looking string hammocks before, but she had never tried to get into one. She and Holly created quite an amusing sight as they discovered how awkward it was to climb into the hammock, trying to settle down without crashing into each other. Even Amelia's sober-looking toddlers gathered around to watch. Amelia finally had to explain by gestures that they were supposed to sleep diagonally—not lengthwise.

When the toddlers of the family tired of watching their guests struggle with the hammock, they retreated into the other room. Chan and Amelia stayed in the room, still silent, and Liz and Holly exchanged impatient whispers, wondering when they would be alone so that they could discuss their predicament. Manuel had disappeared right after dinner and had not yet returned.

'You don't think he's deserted us?' Liz asked.

'I fear that he may be misleading us,' Holly said.

Liz had just begun to get the knack of the hammock when a squawking chicken burst into the tiny room, did a little aimless dance, and dropped directly under her. Something was clearly wrong with the animal, but it took Liz a second to figure out what: the bird's head was dangling from its neck by a single strand of flesh, and what she had first taken to be a red band round its throat was actually the bloody stump of its neck. Just

161

as Liz shrieked, Amelia darted across the room, picked up the chicken's body, and disappeared.

'Let me out of here,' Liz muttered. 'This place is really weird.'

'I, for one, am not going anywhere,' Holly said firmly. 'That chicken is no doubt for us, and I could use some good meat after eating beans and corncake all day.'

'But. . .' Liz sputtered. 'You mean you're going to eat that thing after she killed it right here in the house?'

'Of course. You act as though you never saw anyone kill a chicken before.'

'I never did.'

Holly looked incredulous, then thoughtful. 'I bet Melville—your father, I mean—has seen people kill chickens. How is it that you never accompanied him on any of his journeys here? It is not like in my day when travel was so difficult.'

'Mum thinks that Danny and I should have a normal life. You know, school, piano lessons, and all that stuff.'

Holly did not know but decided not to answer.

Liz went on glumly. 'I wish I were having a more normal life right now. Maybe it was a big mistake coming down here without getting in touch with Mum.'

'What could your mother do to help us now?' Holly fidgeted, sending the hammock swinging. 'I know. We shall write a secret message—like Major André.'

'Who's he?'

'Major André was a British spy who carried the plans to the American fort at West Point during the War of Independence. He had the documents hidden in his riding boot, I think. He was captured and executed by the Yankees.'

'Great. Can't you think of any more inspiring examples?'

'Do not be fainthearted, Liz. Perhaps it did not work for him, but it is still a good idea. We shall write a message saying that we are headed for Tikal. . .that we are being kidnapped and need help. We can hide it in my shoe, and if Manuel does turn out to be reliable, we do not have to use it. If we have trouble, a written message might be our only hope for getting help.'

162

'You're right, Holly. I remember Dad saying that both Mexico and Guatemala have regular patrols on the river. We'll have to stop for food and water along the way, too. There might be a way of getting a letter to the authorities...Oh, Holly, but the letter will have to be in Spanish?'

'You will think of something,' Holly said confidently. 'But first, we need paper and a pencil.'

As quietly as possible Liz eased her way out of the hammock and began to tiptoe across the dirt floor of the hut. it was pitch dark now, and she could hear the sound of snoring in the next room. Her suitcase, she remembered, had been left resting against the wall just inside the main door of the hut. Carefully she felt her way into the main room. As her eyes adjusted to the faint light, she could make out the silhouettes of two extra-large hammocks slung across the far end of the room. Amelia, Chan, and the youngest baby were asleep in one; the other children were piled into the second. She took another step. No one stirred. Encouraged, Liz made her way towards the door and began groping for her luggage. There it was! She gingerly picked up the suitcase. She was just lifting it into her arms when, suddenly, a hand clamped around her ankle!

'Going some place, señorita?'

Liz looked down and saw Manuel's face grinning up at her. Paralyzed with fear, she couldn't answer. Manuel did not let go.

'I was just going to the bathroom, I mean to the outhouse...'

'With this?' Manuel asked, pointing to the luggage.

'I needed something...uh, the soap.'

'Bueno. Take it. But remember, to go somewhere in this country without Manuel is not healthy. To you or to your friend. Understand?'

With that Manuel released his hold on her ankle, and Liz grabbed the pack and hurried out. As she climbed back into the hammock, she saw Holly's ashen face. For the first time Liz realized that Holly was as frightened as she was. She reached out and put her arms around her. There would be no letter writing tonight; they might as well try to get some sleep.

Chapter 18

Friday, December 1

When the girls awoke the next morning, Amelia silently offered them hot tortillas and beans while she went back to the task of packing pieces of roast chicken wrapped in leaves into a bag that was obviously intended for their lunch. As she toyed with her tortillas, Liz admitted to herself that the prospect of eating the chicken no longer seemed quite so disgusting as it had last night.

'No like beans?'

Liz looked up, startled to find Chan grinning at her. 'I speak little English?' he added, making the remark into a question. Chan glanced over his shoulder nervously. 'Manuel he say no talk to you. He say you bad girls. But I talk. Is okay?'

'Terrific,' Liz said. 'Of course it's okay.'

'I like bad girls much,' Chan added.

Holly was about to set Chan straight, but Liz heard a sound outside the cabin door and motioned for her to be quiet.

A few seconds later Manuel entered. 'Time to go, señoritas. Tomorrow you will be in Guatemala. *Vámonos.*'

'Where to now?' Liz asked.

'To the airfield,' replied Manuel. 'The pilot is waiting. This morning you will see the great rapids and the gorge of the

164

Usumacinta. The whole trip will be worth that sight. It's impassable by boat. That is why you have to fly.'

'This is better,' said Holly with satisfaction when she saw the small blue and white Cessna on the Tenosique airstrip. 'I can see how something like this might fly, not those big things we have been on before.'

The pilot, a fat, swarthy man in an open white shirt and blue pants, greeted Manuel with a gold-glinted smile. He nodded pleasantly at the girls as they all climbed inside the craft. Liz and Holly first, since they were to sit in back, then Manuel, and finally, the pilot. All buckled in, the pilot donned one-way sunglasses, worked competently at the controls, waved at the airfield attendant, and took the plane upwards, engine roaring.

Tenosique fell behind; the wide ribbon of the Usumacinta turned below as they banked and circled to the west.

'We must go west a few minutes—towards Palenque—so we won't cross the corner of Guatemala,' yelled Manuel over the engine din. 'We then cross those hills and follow the west side of the river to Yaxchilán,' he added, pointing to the foggy ridge to the left.

The plane, bumping and roaring in the unstable air, lost the river briefly, gained altitude and stability, and moved almost imperceptibly over the trackless forest below. Suddenly the trees were closer—an incredible tangle of monstrous broccoli spears in all possible shades of green. They were above the steep ridge. A few moments later the bottom dropped out, or at least that's the way it seemed. The gorge of the Usumacinta surged into view below.

'Look to the left and straight down,' yelled Manuel.

'Really neat!' cried Liz. 'I never saw anything like *that*.'

Holly could only stare, speechless.

Below them lay the river, a silver trickle now, between sheer cliffs of towering limestone so close together they seemed almost to touch.

'I can see why it is best to fly at times.' Holly said.

Soon after the gorge the pilot bent to the controls, and the plane seemed to brake in the sky and begin its descent. Around another huge hill the grassy airstrip suddenly appeared. The Cessna lined up with it, the engine became almost quiet, and the small plane descended into the forest. Three thumps, a final roar, and they had arrived. Yaxchilán.

'The ruins are over there,' Manuel volunteered. 'Enjoy them until the boatman comes. I will pay the pilot and follow shortly.'

'This was a real lost city,' said Liz as the trail entered the shadowy forest. 'Dad often told me it is almost his favourite ruin. For years it lay here in the jungle,' she remembered, 'with moss all over the stelae and some of the prettiest buildings anywhere. At least that's how it was before the archaeologists started clearing it.'

In the first clearing lay several wooden houses with high pitched thatched roofs. Several naked children played in a huge mud puddle while some taunted a black and white duck that had suddenly appeared. Four skinny brown dogs came whining and barking up to the girls.

'Let us go the other way,' pleaded Holly. 'It seems more interesting.'

The trail up the hill seemed to take an eternity. Holly and Liz clambered up the slippery dirt, over stones that were parts of ruined buildings and terraces, and up steep banks covered with underbrush. Suddenly a huge building appeared before them, a building of stone. Men were working in and around it.

'Look, Holly,' Liz exclaimed. 'They *are* working here. Archaeologists, I mean. Probably from Mexico City.'

The girls sidled quietly over to several men who, shirtless and sweating, were carefully removing dirt and rubble from a long row of squarish stones that appeared to form a huge step in front of the structure. Others were taking the accumulated dirt in wheelbarrows down a trail into the trees.

'Luckily that trail is downhill,' Holly giggled.

'Look,' cried Liz. 'There are pictures and glyphs carved on that big stair. That man there with the clipboard is drawing them. That must be why all these strings are up here—to help him measure and get his drawing right.'

Before they could see the drawing or get closer, Manuel came up behind them.

'You move fast, señoritas.' He grinned. 'I thought you had gone home. The boatman is waiting for us. He will get us to Sayaxché tomorrow night.'

Chapter 19

*S*lowly the long dugout fought its way upstream against the flow of the Usamacinta River, the sputtering old outboard motor whining in protest. The great bend where Yaxchilán lay hidden had passed astern hours ago. The river now wound through a forest so tangled that even the banks were invisible. Occasional long vistas of water led to towering ceiba trees—the holy tree of the Maya. The great trees seemed to grow in places where they could be seen the longest. Most of their branching foliage was filled with dark starbursts of orchid plants and some with flocks of resting, brightly coloured macaws that broke into flight as the boat neared their silent world. Glistening turtles crowded logs against the river's edge. Beyond lay the shadowy world of the trackless jungle.

'This must have been what it was like before there were people,' Holly observed, gazing at the formidable desolation.

Liz nodded in agreement.

The boat was a wonder in itself. It must have weighed a ton. Yet it cut the water cleanly, if slowly, as boats like it had for more than a thousand years on this very river. Now, instead of Maya rowers, the thirty-foot craft held only the girls, Manuel, and Ramón, a morose young boatman who had come from Sayaxché to meet them. In the bottom of the dugout lay a crate of warm Coca-Colas, plastic bottles of water, a burlap sack of God-knows-what, some tattered tarpaulins, and three gasoline cans that would surely qualify as antiques.

Liz wondered who the boat boy was and how he and Manuel knew each other. If the boy was afraid of Manuel, he certainly didn't show it. While Manuel presided silently over the motor in the stern of the dugout, Ramón's spirits seemed to lift, and he started a running monologue describing the strange plants and animals that they were passing, explaining how the dugout had been carved out of a solid mahogany log, and asking questions about America. Ramón's language was a makeshift mixture of English and Spanish with a few Maya words thrown in. Liz couldn't understand all they said, perhaps it was for the best, Liz figured, since Holly's garbled explanations of the modern world would merely confirm Ramón's low opinion of female intelligence.

Manuel, meanwhile, seemed to be growing bored with their chatter. He reached into the string bag containing their lunch and pulled out a few tortillas. 'You want to see something, señoritas? Look, I show you.' And with that he threw a tortilla into the placid water. A sudden movement! The steady ripple of the wake broke with a splash...an enormous alligator snatched the tortilla! Then the water resettled.

Manuel laughed. 'This is not their favourite food. The best is food that moves.'

This statement was accompanied by a meaningful glance that left even Ramón speechless. But to her own surprise Liz felt much less frightened than she had been the night before. It occurred to her that if Manuel had wanted to rob or kill her and Holly, he had already had many chances to do so. There was no reason to bring them all this way and certainly no reason to involve Chan and his family. Since it was obvious by now that Manuel wasn't just an ordinary, cut-rate guide, he must have some reason for wanting to deliver them safely to Tikal.

But why? How could he have known she and Holly were even coming to Guatemala? It can't be Wilkins, she thought.

He *tried* to talk us out of going...

Then, in a flash, she saw the whole picture. Wilkins had only made it *seem* as if he wanted them to stay away. Not only had he been upset by the idea that she and Holly might try to go to Tikal on their own, he had seemed angry and defensive at the suggestion that her father might still be alive. And they had moved right into his trap! But what were his reasons for wanting them there? She decided not to worry Holly about it until she knew more.

The darkness grew deeper and the river became a silver road through the blackness.

'Señoritas,' Manuel said. clambering over the gear as he approached the girls in the front of the boat. 'Soon we will be entering the mouth of the Pasión River to get to Sayaxché. It is there, on the east bank where the two rivers join, that the Guatemalan soldiers have a military station—Pipiles. It is like a checkpoint. Luckily the river is wide there. We will have to keep to the opposite bank and try to work the boat across the stream into the Pasión without the lookouts seeing us. Since you have no papers, it would be very bad should we be stopped—bad for you and for me. Soon now, Ramón will cover the motor with the sacks he has brought so as to cut down on the noise. Once we reach safety, I will tell you. Say nothing from now on.'

In an hour that seemed an eternity Manuel spotted a tiny light off the port bow. Pipiles. The river was wide, but not wide enough.

Not *nearly* wide enough, Liz thought, crawling beneath the dark smelly tarpaulin she hoped would protect her.

Slowly the boat edged along the opposite bank, and fairly quietly. Liz thought she heard men laughing and yelling, but the sound soon died away. Sunken twigs and brambles scraped the rough bottom of the dugout. If just one caught the propeller and the motor were to stop, the waters would send them straight to the bank and dock where the soldiers were.

Another hour passed. Suddenly the silence was broken. 'It is safe now, señoritas,' whispered Manuel. 'You can come out now. We will camp soon at an abandoned shelter on the bank of the Pasión River. Welcome to Guatemala!'

169

Saturday, December 2

A bright day. The blue Guatemalan sky was mirrored perfectly in the strong, quiet waters of the Pasión. The boat, refuelled, made steady headway towards Sayaxché.

Here it did not seem so desolate. Frequent farmsteads and large clearings broke the monotony, and other canoes appeared on the river. But Liz felt even more alone as the enormity of her and Holly's predicament dawned upon her.

We're caught, she told herself again. How could I have been such a dunce? I must get help soon.

Holly broke into her thoughts. 'Liz, I must confess that your garb is better suited than mine for these travels.' If the rest of the journey was to be more arduous than this, Holly feared she might be ill equipped for it. 'I should have purchased more rugged clothing when you did. As my mother used to say, "Where sense is wanting, everything is wanting." '

'Another quoter in the family?' Liz said. 'Anyway, Holly, that one I can solve. Here. Put on a pair of jeans and one of the shirts. But I don't know where we can get you hiking shoes now.'

'My footwear is sturdy enough, I think. I shall retain my

sunbonnet. Truly a proper garment for here!'

There would be one stop before Sayaxché—to buy fuel and to gain time—for Manuel wanted to arrive after dark at the small town, 'so as not to attract too much attention,' he had said, grinning.

Almost as soon as the canoe docked and after Manuel had gone for fuel at a nearby compound, Liz and Holly retreated to a sheltered place out of sight of the small settlement. Holly changed. The final effect was startling: the sunbonnet still firmly in place, its streamers reaching to the flap pockets of the shirt.

'At least you're over halfway twentieth century now,' Liz said.

Holly smoothed the jeans with her hands and smiled. 'It is not as pretty but it *is* more practical.'

Liz reached into her pack for paper and a pen, and scrawled a short note: 'I am Professor Melville Dutton's daughter. Look for me at Sean Wilkins's camp at Tikal, Guatemala.'

Liz wanted to translate the note into Spanish, but the language came no easier for her than it ever had. Finally she wrote in big block letters the words, AYUDE POR FAVOR and IMPORTANTE. That was as close as she could come to 'Help!' and it would have to do. After folding the note and hiding it in her boot, Liz led Holly back to the boat. 'Now we have to find someone who can help us,' she said.

Holly nodded in Ramón's direction. 'He has been friendly to us. Can you make him understand our plight?'

'Maybe, if Manuel stays away long enough.' She walked up to the boatman. 'Ramón,' she said, choosing her words carefully, 'would you help me and Holly if we were in danger?'

'*Claro*...of course,' Ramón replied boastfully. 'Almost I am a man now. Very strong.'

Liz tried another tack. 'Manuel is not a good man.'

Ramón looked serious. '*Es mejicano*...Mexican.'

This, Liz knew, was Ramón's way of saying that Manuel was not a Maya Indian and, therefore, not very trustworthy in his eyes. But if he knew more, he clearly wasn't eager to say so.

'Ramón, will you take a message for me to the police? Very

171

important. Manuel is taking us to his boss, someone who is a very bad man, and we may be in danger.'

'I tell. They no believe,' Ramón said fatalistically.

Liz reached into her pack and pulled out her mother's credit cards and letter. She had almost no money left, but these weren't going to do her much good here on the Usumacinta. 'Here,' she told Ramón, 'if they don't believe you, give them these.'

'Okay. I try. In Sayaxché. Pretty good police there. Army police.' Ramón took the note, the letter, and the credit cards and stuffed them inside his shirt. 'We no talk now,' he said softly, pointing up the path where Manuel had just appeared on his way back to the boat.

'Do you believe that the army will come to our assistance?' Holly asked, swatting at mosquitoes. 'We are not even natives of this country, and we did slip by them after all.'

'If they realize who we are—who my father is, rather—I think they will. He's very well known in Sayaxché. He was before he got lost, I mean.' Liz stared glumly into the fire. 'I only hope that Ramón is luckier than Major André.'

When there was just enough light to guide the boat through the submerged obstacle course of drowned trees and hidden sandbanks, the four departed for Sayaxché.

Liz heard it first—the throb of a big engine in the darkness. It awoke her from a worried sleep of alligator dreams and dark whirlpools.

'The ferry at Sayaxché muttered Manuel. 'The town is on the right and so are the *officiales*. On the left is the road to Flores and Tikal. A truck is waiting. I will lead you to it. You will conceal yourselves in the back and remain silent. This is our last obstacle.'

The road from Sayaxché to Flores was filled with bruising ruts and potholes, and the driver kept the ancient and cumbersome vehicle so far to one side that two tyres rode on the bushes and brambles that edged the road. 'It is not as rough a ride that way,' Manuel joked.

Yet, somehow, they slept through Flores while the fateful journey continued toward a goal they did not yet know.

Chapter 21

*J*ust after sunrise. Holly awakened Liz. 'Look,' she said, pointing to the immense roof combs of the Tikal pyramid temples. Holly could not help gasping in admiration. 'It is the Hanging Gardens of Babylon and the Tower of Babel all in one place,' she cried.

'More like Daniel getting thrown into the lion's den, if you ask me,' Liz said, too worrried to share Holly's exitement.

'No *leones* in this jungle, señorita,' Manuel laughed. 'Only jaguars.'

'And snakes,' Liz added.

'*Sí, sí, muchas culebras,*' Manuel agreed, unaware that Liz had been referring to him.

It was still early morning when the truck swung around a corner in the narrow road just as another truck—a small one carrying four jungle rangers who were now being relieved of their duty—was pulling away for the Jungle Inn. The rangers were laughing and slapping each other on the back. Manuel cursed and floored the accelerator.

173

The further they'd come, the more worried Liz had been getting. By now, though she still felt the only way to find her father was through Wilkins, the prospect of encountering him had her terrified. It seemed to her that the rangers in the truck might be the last friendly faces·she'd see, and she suddenly felt an urgency to leave some last clue or trail with them. She turned to Holly, and Holly seemed to read her mind. They both craned their necks upwards and waved at the truck with wide, sweeping gestures. The rangers stared at them, then waved happily back. 'It's no use,' Liz said. 'They think we're just being friendly. But at least they saw us, and maybe they'll remember our faces.'

Manuel swung the truck onto a barely visible side road and ground to a halt just as Sean Wilkins emerged from his tent.

'Why, Miss Dutton!' Wilkins said cheerfully. 'Once again you've proved me wrong. How in the world were you and your little friend able to manage?'

'In the Dutton family,' Liz said icily, 'we can manage anything we put our minds to. Besides, we had a good deal of help.'

'The señoritas were very brave, very valorous,' Manuel added, now all smiles.

'Your *friend*, Mr Rojas, was exceedingly eager to bring us here,' Holly said.

'Oh, yes, Rojas, good work,' Wilkins said, unruffled. 'Well, young ladies, there's no use wasting any time. It's true that I wanted you to come here. In fact, I intend to help you in your quest. You see, I, too, believe that Mel Dutton is alive.'

'You do?' Liz squealed, unable to restrain herself.

'Not only do I believe it, but I am convinced that you can help me find him. No one else has your conviction. Not even your own mother. You represent the last hope of bringing your father out of that jungle alive.'

Whatever Liz had been expecting from Wilkins, this was not it. Thrown off balance by his revelation that he felt her father was indeed alive, she could see no alternative but to follow him inside the tent. Glancing uncertainly at Holly, she shrugged her shoulders and ducked under the canvas door flap. Holly followed, most wary about the situation. Wilkins's offer of breakfast made them both feel better. Except for Amelia's roast chicken, their fare since leaving Mexico City had consisted mainly of cold tortillas, black beans, onions, and chili peppers alternated with hot tortillas and black beans. Now, despite their distrust of Wilkins, Liz and Holly couldn't help munching enthusiastically on the hard-boiled eggs and fresh fruit Wilkins set before them. By the time they had finished their meal, the girls were almost willing to consider the possibility that this man might be on their side after all.

'...I know this will be difficult for you to accept, Miss Elizabeth,' Wilkins began as soon as breakfast was cleared away, 'but your father was eager to claim sole credit for the major new Maya site he was about to locate. His decision to wander off into the jungle without a radio and without leaving me specific instructions as to his plans was highly unusual. This is dangerous country. All kinds of accidents might have befallen your father, and there is always the possibility that he met with foul play. The *chicleros* are well aware of the value of Maya artifacts and there have been cases of violence in the past. So until I spoke with you in New Orleans, I had come to agree with the opinion of my colleagues that your father must be long dead. Then, after talking with you and Miss Holly, I began to ask myself, "If there were any hope of Mel Dutton's being alive, where would that hope lie?"'

'Yes, where?' Liz asked impatiently.

'Why, at the lost Jaguar city, of course. If your father did succeed in finding the city, I'm afraid he would again be tempted to keep the information to himself. He'd want to explore and describe the ruins as completely as possible, rather than calling in his colleagues, such as myself, who would then share credit for the discovery...and the possibility of some hidden treasure...even gold.'

'But the jungle was searched thoroughly last summer...' Liz interjected.

'There's no such thing as a thorough search in this area. Such an enterprise might take a thousand years. But if we knew where the Jaguar city was located...your father might be ill, hurt...anything could have happened by now. Surely the time for secrecy, if there ever was one, is past.'

'But you said that we held the key, Mr Wilkins. In what respect?' Holly asked.

'The jaguar pendant,' Wilkins said. 'I cannot be certain that it will help us to find Mel Dutton alive, but I believe it might. I'd like to show it to the *chicleros* around here. They might know something of its origins. Perhaps they could lead us to where it was found.'

'Mr Wilkins, I have one question,' Holly began slowly.

'Yes, yes?'

'What is a *"chiclero"*?'

Wilkins smiled. 'A *"chiclero"*, Miss Holly, is a man who gathers gum resins from the sapodilla trees. The resin, known as chicle, is the basis for chewing gum. This chicle earns him a good income by local standards, and so he guards his route jealously. But *chicleros* know the jungle as few others do. They make excellent guides.'

Holly looked deep in thought as Liz slowly removed the jaguar pendant from the thong around her neck. 'Here you are, Mr Wilkins,' she said. 'I still don't know what this pendant means, but if it can help find my father alive, you might as well have it.'

'A wise decision,' Wilkins answered, carefully slipping the pendant into his jacket pocket. 'Now, perhaps you young ladies would like to take a look at Temple IV, the structure that Mel Dutton spent so much time studying. I'll go ask Manuel to accompany us. You see, the ruins will be closed to tourists all this week due to the failure of fresh water supplies at the inn. Water is always scarce during the dry season, but this is highly unusual. It seems that last night someone vandalized the pump room.'

Wilkins departed in search of Manuel, and Holly stared at Liz in dismay. 'I do not think it was wise to give him that pendant. He has been trying to take it from you ever since he first beheld it. Why do you trust him with it now?'

'I don't, but I don't care anymore. If he can find Dad alive, what else matters? Anyway, if he really wants the pendant, what's to stop him from taking it? You heard him. We're all alone her. The ruins are closed.'

'Well, he spoke truly about one thing,' Holly said. 'He knows a lot about chicle. Come here, I'll show you.'

Taking Liz by the hand, she hurried out of the tent and into the clearing near where Manuel had parked the truck. 'I caught a glimpse of this as we arrived.'

Holly pointed towards a large wooden packing crate stencilled with the legend: ICRAR U. S./CHICLE. The crate had not yet been nailed shut.

Unable to resist, Liz lifted the loose wooden lid and peered inside. There were objects wrapped in banana leaves. She tore at one package. Staring back at her was a pair of bulging, grotesquely crossed eyes and an open leering mouth. Liz jumped. 'That's no chicle, that's for sure.'

'It looks like a mask!' Holly exclaimed, peering inside. 'It is. Remember that jade mosaic mask we saw in the museum? The crossed eyes symbolize the sun god. I read that in the book we saw in Professor Goodman's office. It must be very valuable. Not many such masks have ever been discovered. One came from Tikal.'

'Very good, Miss Holly. You're quite a scholar.' Sean Wilkins had approached so noiselessly that once again both girls were startled. Surprisingly, however, he seemed more amused than angry at their snoopng.

'If you have finished examining our camp, perhaps you'd now like to see the temple I told you about,' he suggested.

'Sure, Mr Wilkins, we'd love to,' Liz sputtered. 'But first I think we should send a telegram to my mother to let her know where we are. She'll be so thrilled that you think Dad might be alive after all.'

'Don't be naïve, Elizabeth. Do you think Manuel went to all this trouble to bring you here by an untraceable route for nothing?'

Liz opened her mouth to answer. She never had a chance. The sound caught in her throat as a large and very grimy hand descended from behind and clamped itself firmly across her mouth! As Liz struggled frantically, she saw that Manuel had a furious Holly by the arm. Holly was too quick for him. With a twist she escaped his grasp and began running towards the road.

'Holly, go!' Liz screamed, surprised to hear the sound of her own voice ring out. Her captor had removed his hand to tie her wrists with a thick, dirty rope.

'Hold her still, damn you. Do you want me to break this off in her arm?' Sean Wilkins jabbed a hypodermic into her tricep, and almost immediately Liz felt waves of numbness advancing the length of her arm. The last thing she saw before the heavy blanket descended over her head was Holly being dragged back into the clearing by a raging Manuel.

'Careful with that one,' Wilkins laughed. 'There's something strange about her.'

Manuel grunted something unintelligible in reply, and Liz felt herself slipping into unconsciousness. Her final impression was of the overpowering smell of the blanket. It was sweet—rather like the smell of chewing gum.

*L*ess than ten miles away from Sean Wilkins's camp, Professor Melville Dutton and Jorge Lopez finished setting up the makeshift camp, a safe distance off the trail leading south from Uaxactún. The afternoon light was turning yellow and the shadows of late afternoon were now beginning to blend in the surrounding jungle. Hot, still air lay heavily in the sun-dappled clearings.

Ordinarily this was Mel Dutton's favourite time of day—the time to wash away the dirt and fatigue of the trail and relax, to put the events of the day in order and make plans for the next. Today, however, he felt an uncanny tenseness. Dutton sat on a burlap carton near his tent, almost oblivious to the chatter of a band of spider monkeys that had suddenly broken the silence and were unwittingly taunting a large bushmaster snake. He motioned deftly to Jorge, who also acknowledged the presence of the dangerous snake.

Balancing the case and notebook on his lap, Dutton began writing a letter to his longtime colleague, Herschel Goodman:

December 3

Dear Herschel,

Ever since late August when Jorge came back to camp and told me the unbelievable — that Wilkins had murdered Raul for not killing _me_ — I have scarcely dared to move from my hiding spot. I really feel alone. It's hell to be out here without contact with my colleagues, and without my notes and library. But since I have no way of knowing which of the searchers are in Wilkins's pay, I have not risked showing myself to a_ny_ of them. I will _not_, therefore, return to Tikal until I can be sure that, whatever happens to me, you will know all the clues I now have as to the location of the lost Jaguar City. Perhaps you can save it from Wilkins's depredations.

By my calculations, the date on the new stela fragment from near Temple IV

records the Eighth Katun anniversary of
the earlier date 9.9.14.12.4 9 Kan 17 Ceh.
   That very date, 9 Kan 17 Ceh, appears
on the jade jaguar pendant:

   Now this date, Herschel, deals with a
Venus event.   I believe that on that

date 9.9.14.12.4, which
I equate to October 28,
A.D. 627, Venus rose in
a line made by the location of the
Jaguar City — itself recorded on both the
pendant and the stela fragment by the
glyphs:

PENDANT   STELA

   In order to firmly establish that alignment, a third point is necessary.

That elusive third point is, I'm certain now, none other than Temple IV at Tikal!

Granted, the temple and its pyramid were built some 160 years after A.D. 627 but, since the same Venus event is recorded on the later stela, it appears that the Maya kept the knowledge of this alignment over the years and perhaps re-marked it with that stela. If that is true, I must now depend on Venus!

VENUS AT RISING

HORIZON

JAGUAR CITY ON THIS LINE

TEMPLE IV

I cannot list for you the recurrences of this sight line since I don't have my astronomical tables with me. But the Venus cycle of 584 days and the Maya day designation 9 Kan 17 Ceh come together, or coincide, every 37,960 days, or about 104 years. Therefore, if the alignment of Temple IV, the Jaguar City, and the rising of Venus occurred on October 28, 687, it would repeat in 731, 835, 939, etc. By my calculations here, the event happened most recently late in 1874. The next happening will be at dawn tomorrow morning, December 4, 1978, and I must be on Temple IV to get the reading, for another chance will not be available until November 28, A.D. 2082!

For supporting evidence of all this, Herschel, please look again at another fragment from near Temple IV in Maler's photograph in

the old Peabody Museum publication —
I cannot recall the volume number.
Anyway, it bears a "count-forward" test
with an interval of 3.0.10.14.0, or
435,880 days. Now the clincher — if
you take the fragment I found — dated
9.17.14.12.4 6 Kan 7 Chen and add
the 435,880 days to it, you arrive at
12.18.5.8.4, which AGAIN equates to
December 4, 1978! And, of all things,
a 'cracked earth' event is
predicted for that day, which,
of course, is tomorrow! Soon we will
know for sure just how good the Maya
were at their predictions.

So, if I am not at the temple tomorrow morning to make the critical
sighting, I will never have another
chance. And if I fail, Wilkins
will certainly discover the Jaguar City

and plunder it before responsible archaeologists get to it. We must face the
fact that there are big money interests
organizing the systematic looting of Maya
ruins. This is no amateur game and
even if I can manage to get Wilkins
behind bars, the Jaguar City will not be
safe until we can set up a guard station
there.

As soon as I have taken the sighting
tomorrow, I plan to leave the Petén by a
secret route Jorge and I have arranged
with Clarence Macomber. Because I am
not sure that I will escape alive, I
am giving you as much information as
I can in this letter. I know that,
whatever happens to me, Jorge will find
a way to deliver it. Please see that
he is well rewarded some day.

In haste, Mel

Mel Dutton read over the letter carefully, sealed it, and handed it to Jorge who immediately placed it inside his shirt. Before turning back toward Flores, the young man embraced his tall red-haired friend and bade him good luck in the Maya language. Although he did not mention it, Jorge was deeply worried about Dutton's safety. Only last night he had dreamed that he would never see the archaeologist again. As Jorge cut his way back along the narrow jungle path, he reviewed the plan he and Mel Dutton had worked out so carefully. Everything had been accounted for except for chance—and that, reflected Jorge, was in the hands of the gods.

Jorge was right, of course. And it was pure chance that a *chiclero* named Emiliano Guzmán happened to be crouched in the high branches of a mahogany tree, scanning the landscape for sapodillas, in the path of Jorge's cautious approach through the jungle. Recognizing Jorge as his chance for a fat reward from Sean Wilkins, Emiliano climbed down the straight trunk until he hung motionless just fifteen feet above the trail. The jungle canopy was so dense that not even an alert woodsman like Jorge could notice that he was being watched. Yet Emiliano managed to aim his machete so accurately that it found a clear path through the heavy vines. Jorge had just an instant to react to the sound of something moving in the trees above him. The moment was long enough for him to wonder whether his assailant was jaguar or man, but as he raised his eyes to find out, the machete crashed into his forehead, splitting his skull as easily as if it had been a ripe coconut.

*L*iz Dutton opened her eyes to the rays of the tropical sunset streaming through a tiny opening far above her head. Her arm was throbbing with pain. Reflexively she raised her hand to rub her aching right arm, then looked down in surprise, realizing that her hands were no longer tied.

'You might at least say thank you,' a voice said, and Liz raised her head to see Holly, cheerfully brandishing the severed rope in one hand and a wicked-looking hunting knife in the other.

'Holly!' Liz cried. 'Where are we? And where did you get that knife?'

'One question at a time,' Holly said quite cheerfully. 'The knife was donated by our friend over here.' Liz turned in response to Holly's wave of the hand. Liz opened her mouth to scream again, but Holly stopped her. There, slouched against the walls of the stone chamber, was Raúl Uc, or what remained of him, which was not much besides a skeleton and a few shreds of disintegrated clothing.

'Hush, my friend, though I doubt that anyone can hear us here,' she added. 'Still we must take no chances. It is only one of the dear departed. You act as though you have never seen a dead person before.'

'I never have,' Liz gasped.

'In my day sudden death was not uncommon. I saw two baby brothers taken by the fever in my own house.' Holly looked pensive for a second, then stood up, decisively changing the subject. 'I must say, though, I never appreciated the truth of the saying "ashes to ashes, dust to dust" before now. Fortunately the gentleman's knife was more durable than he. While you were sleeping, I was able to make good use of it. It is our good fortune that Rojas tied my hands in front of me, not behind like yours, or I do not think I could have managed.'

Liz pulled her half-numb body into a sitting position, then slowly began shaking her hands and feet to restore the circulation. 'Great work, Holly,' she said at last. 'Now how are we going to get out of here? Where's the door?'

'That is what our silent companion here probably wanted to know,' Holly giggled, but this time she did not succeed in concealing the panic in her voice.

Liz looked around her in the dim light, trying to ignore the terrible dark shape of the skeletel remains. The room they were in was long and narrow—so narrow, in fact, that Liz, standing in the centre, could almost touch the side walls with both arms outstretched. The floor was uneven and very slippery, for the dirt and rubble had fallen or filtered in over centuries, slowly covering what must have been the original floor below.

Both ends of the room ended in vertical walls of carefully laid stone blocks that extended upwards into darkness. The side walls rose vertically, too, but only about the the girls' eye level, where a horizontal layer of narrow slabs projected slightly into the room. Above that course of dark, damp masonry lay another to form the vaulting. Each succeeding layer of stone projected further inward so as to create two walls that slanted toward one another, narrowing the open space in between. These vault walls stopped just short of meeting in the darkness above. There the ancient builders had simply capped the

High at one end a tiny shaft of light shone into the dark hollow of
the crypt, emphasized by the stream of rising dust particles. 'It's
a Maya room,' Liz remarked. 'Dad told me that the old architects never developed the true arch. This was their version.'

narrow slot with great slabs of limestone. High at one end a tiny shaft of light shone into the dark hollow of the crypt, emphasized by the stream of rising dust particles.

'It's a Maya room,' Liz remarked. 'Dad told me that the old architects never developed the true arch. This was their version.'

'Did your father ever mention how one might get *out* of a Maya room?' Holly asked tartly.

Liz shook her head sadly.

'There has to be a way, and we have to find it,' Holly said. 'Let us look at the whole room very carefully. Maybe we will see our answer.'

'Our bags are not in here.' Liz said.

Reaching into her khaki shirt pocket, Holly said, 'Fortunately I have my mirror.'

'What if no one finds us until we're already dead?' Liz said with a shudder. 'Hurry, Holly.'

Holly's mirror caught the small shaft of light that cut into the room from the tiny hole above. Slowly, using the light reflected from the mirror, they scanned the room, making a shaky but determined path along the stones and gradually working upward into the shadow of the vault. Liz followed with her eyes. First the walls. Not much there—except for an occasional stone slightly shifted and hundreds of whitish rootlets invading the narrow cracks between the blocks. Some areas still bore patches of old plaster and showed traces of red paint that had once revealed the lower walls.

'Nothing, nothing,' Liz muttered as her eyes and the reflected beam continued their systematic scan upwards.

'Wait,' Liz said suddenly. 'Go back a bit. There. No, it's only an old wooden beam crossing the vault. There's part of another one just beyond it. Go on.

'Stop again, Holly.' Liz need not have said anything, for Holly's light had already stopped. It rested quivering on one of the central capstones. painted on it was a large red circle.

'What can that be?' Holly asked. 'Does it help?'

'Maybe,' replied Liz, her excitement growing. 'Dad once told me of a tomb that was found here. It had a spot on the ceiling like this one. He thought maybe it was the last capstone put in place—in some kind of a weird ceremony. If so, it should be the easiest capstone to get out. I'll just bet that Wilkins knows about such things from all his looting, and that's how he and Manuel put us in here. Let's try. It looks like our only chance.'

'Now all we have to do,' Holly said, 'is to find out how to climb all the way up there. We have a knife. Let us dig out some stones from this debris and start a pyramid of our own—a pile of rubble in the middle of the floor. We can at least reach that old beam, pull the other one out of the wall, and try to push the capstone out.'

The two girls set to work.

That evening, Clarence Macomber sat at a corner table at the crowded *cantina* in Flores, nursing a beer and wondering what to do next. He was supposed to meet Jorge shortly after midday to collect a letter and make final arrangements to help Mel Dutton cross the border into Belize the next day. But Jorge had failed to appear, and Clarence was sure something was very wrong. Yet when he had met with Dutton at the secret location in the jungle two weeks before to arrange his passage out of the country, the archaeologist had been adamant about not wanting the police brought in under any circumstances. The authorities would not be likely to understand the importance of Dutton's being at the temple tomorrow, and it was vital that they did not interfere.

Now, however, Clarence was not so sure. If the professor wanted to take such risks, that was his business. He had no intention of walking into trouble.

'Clarence, *buenas noches. ¿Qué pasa...*what's up?'

It was Consuela, one of the liveliest and most intelligent of the Flores bar girls, silhouetted against the faded glare of neon signs. Clarence made a point of remaining on good terms with all of the girls at the *cantina*, that was part of the business of being a tourist guide as he saw it, but he really enjoyed talking to Consuela—at least he did normally.

'Sit down, Consuela, 'I'll buy you a beer before I leave.'

Consuela turned down the volume on the blaring jukebox. *'Ay mano,* never have I seen so much business. The Jungle Inn is closed for the week. The tourists, they go to the big hotel, and the help, they are all here.'

'You haven't seen Jorge López by any chance? You know, the good-looking fellow who works for the archaeological expedition at Tikal.'

'Jorge, no,' Consuela said, 'but I see his boss. Yesterday.'

'You mean Professor Dutton? You saw him?'

The girl looked exasperated. 'Professor Dutton is dead, *muerto.* You think I am a witch, consorting with the spirits? I mean Señor Wilkins.'

This was very interesting indeed. Mel Dutton surely hadn't known that Wilkins was coming to Tikal. Wilkins must have just flown in from New Orleans unexpectedly.

Pleased that her news had made an impression, Consuela launched into her tale of Señor Wilkins's surprising visit to the *cantina.* For Mel Dutton to drop into the local watering hole would not have been so unusual, but Sean Wilkins was not known for sociability. When he entered the *cantina* last night, however, it had been obvious to Consuela and everyone else there that he was already somewhat drunk and in an uncharacteristically talkative mood. Consuela had boldly asked him to buy her a drink. Then, she said, he had invited her to sit with him and talk.

Clarence placed a folded paper bill on the table in front of Consuela and returned to studying the label on his beer bottle.

'He talk about the *terroristas.'*

'Terrorists. What terrorists?'

'No sé... I don't know. I think maybe he little bit crazy. He say he leave Tikal soon because of fear of *terroristas.'*

Clarence had heard enough. There was no way of knowing what Sean Wilkins was up to with his talk of terrorists—there were no terrorists for miles around—but Clarence felt sure that Sean Wilkins's visit to Flores had a definite purpose. So if Wilkins was expecting trouble, he himself was likely to be the cause. After flipping a few more *quetzales* onto the metal folding table, Clarence smiled tensely in Consuela's direction and hurried out of the *cantina*.

Whatever was going on here, it was too big a matter for the local police. Clarence ran to his jeep and sped off in the direction of the army post at Sayaxché. He arrived two hours later just in time to interrupt an argument between the sentry and an agitated young boy who kept insisting, without much prospect of success, that he had an important message for the commander. Clarence, who was well known to the sentry, was about to pass on by when he overheard the boy mention a name that sounded like 'Dotón.'

Alarmed, Clarence jumped from his vehicle and examined the credit cards that the boy was vainly trying to call to the sentry's attention.

Monday, December 4

No one in Sean Wilkins's camp had even thought of sleep all night. The arrival of Emiliano Guzmán with the letter he had taken from Jorge's body had thrown Wilkins and his group into a frenzy of desperate planning. The news that Mel Dutton would be on Temple IV in a few hours was almost too good to be true, but it gave Wilkins very little time to get the final stages of his plan in motion. He and Emiliano had spent the last half hour bent intently over the large scale map Wilkins had of the central part of Tikal. The bright white light of the propane lamp glinted on the plastic sheet.

Wilkins now leaned over a smoothed out area of the floor on which he had set several blocks of wood, tin cans, and bits of pottery...all representing the principal architectural and geographical features of Tikal.

'Emiliano,' Wilkins commanded with quiet authority, pointing with his gold ball-point pen, 'you will station yourself here, on the northwest corner of Temple III. We know from the letter that Dutton will be on the east side of Temple IV, so you should be able to see him clearly once it starts getting light. Manuel and I will be concealed in the darkness on the west side of Temple IV, so we will not be able to see him until we come out. I will depend on you, my friend, to watch Dutton's every move with the binoculars—*every* move, *hombre*, for we must know exactly where he takes his sighting from, and Manuel and I might come out too late for that. Do nothing to give your position away until he appears to be finished.

¿*Comprende?* Manuel and I will then confront *el profesor* and make an arrangement—his findings in exchange for the lives of his daughter and the other girl.

'Also,' Wilkins continued, 'there's the matter of the dynamite, Emiliano. Manuel and I have set it in the vault of Temple IV. The activating mechanism is already in place over on Temple III. You will see it under some brush on the northwest corner.'

'But, señor, surely he will agree to save the children's lives? Why must we dynamite the temple?' Emiliano asked, the whine in his voice suggesting that he asked from fear rather than any humane concern.

'Don't be stupid,' Wilkins sneered. 'As soon as we show him the girls and get the information, Manuel and I will shoot all three of them. All you have to do is wait until we've descended into the plaza. Then push the plunger *así*, and the temple's summit will be blown to bits. How else can I be sure that there isn't some other key to the location of the lost city up there?'

Emiliano looked more unhappy than ever but nodded in agreement.

'Do not worry, *hombre*,' Wilkins assured his helper, placing his hand confidently on Emiliano's shoulder. 'I tell you, all of this will be blamed on the *terroristas*. The authorities will receive an anonymous tip making it appear that a terrorist organization takes full credit for the incident. That will serve a double purpose. No one will connect us with the murders and certainly—if I know my tourists and archaeologists—virtually none of them will come to this area for a long while. We will need that time, you see, to get to the Jaguar city without disturbance.'

Briefly reassured, Emiliano nodded. 'The plan seems good,' he agreed. Almost *too* good, he thought to himself.

'Very good, Emiliano,' Wilkins said, rising abruptly. 'Now we must go. Get the light and binoculars. You might bring your rifle too, just in case...'

Manuel Rojas and Sean Wilkins sat quietly in the darkness on their precarious perch on top of Temple IV. For about an hour and a half now they had maintained their vigilance. They were effectively concealed from the east side of the great building by the massive dark shape of the roof comb, the false façade the ancient architects had built on top of the temple to enhance its appearance. Wilkins was hoping that Dutton would appear there, just on the other side of their vantage point. Hoping, too, that Emiliano was in *his* proper position over on Temple III. The cool damp stone was reassuring and solid, Wilkins thought, remembering the tortuous, slippery climb up the gigantic pyramid. Now it was only a matter of

196

waiting while trying not to think of ants or scorpions or the
nearly two hundred feet of darkness that lay between him and
the forest floor below. Carefully he shifted his weight, relieving
a slight cramp, and touched the oiled wood of his gunstock.

Suddenly three quick blinks of light showed from Temple
III. Emiliano was in place, but at a slightly lower level than
Rojas and Wilkins. Would he be able to see clearly enough
from that angle?

'Look, Señor Wilkins,' Manuel whispered. 'The signal!'
Emiliano's light had flashed twice, then paused, then flashed
twice again.

A smile played across Wilkins's face in the darkness.
'Everything's on schedule,' he whispered back with
satisfaction. He looked downward. A second light bobbed
erratically along the trail approaching the front of the base of
Temple IV. 'There he is,' muttered Wilkins contemptuously,

197

'the great Professor Dutton—and probably not even armed.'

Mel Dutton strode as fast as he dared along the familiar trail, his small hooded flashlight picking out the irregularities along the way. He had reached the base of Temple IV and now sought the beginning of the nearly vertical slash of trail that would take him to the summit far above. With a grimace he shifted the cumbersome wooden box strapped to his back which held the heavy surveyor's transit. Dutton checked his watch. Changing the small light to his left hand and shouldering the thick oak tripod with his right—and stronger—hand gave him brief respite. Carefully he laid his hat beside the trail—he would not need it—and, after several deep breaths, resolutely began the climb. Moving like a human fly, he ascended the pyramid towards the stars.

Above, Wilkins began to lose his composure. 'Hurry, man, hurry,' he whispered to no one in particular.

Something large bit him in the soft flesh behind his right knee. He winced, grabbed the khaki cloth of his trousers, and pinched something hard. He squeezed and kneaded the cloth until he was sure he had killed it. He almost let out a cry of pain—gritted his teeth and then managed to shake off the effect of the venom.

Carrying his cumbersome burden, Dutton negotiated the trail with infinite care. The climb up Temple IV was difficult enough in broad daylight with both hands free, and now, in the darkness, it was nearly impossible. Finally Dutton had to place the small light in his mouth, freeing one hand; now if he slipped, he could grab onto one of the small trees that grew from the disarray of stone and rubble that was once the temple staircase. 'But not the wild papaya plants,' he told himself. 'They snap off like balsa wood. That would be a hell of a way to die.'

In twenty minutes Dutton had reached the temple itself. After resting, he inched around it to another slope of rubble that would take him to the roof. For another few minutes his light played against the stone and dirt only inches from his eyes, then shot off into nothingness. He had reached the roof of Temple IV. Oblivious to the presence of two figures barely fifteen feet away, Dutton stood and walked to the flat area in front of the roof comb. Wilkins and Rojas heard his sigh of relief and the brief thumps as he set the transit box and the tripod down on the ancient stucco surface of the temple roof.

Dutton quietly paced the expanse of intact roof, carefully playing his light over every square inch of its surface.

'There's got to be something here,' he said to himself. 'Some clue on just where the Maya would have taken their sighting—if the consolidation work here hasn't obliterated it.' The hunch was a good one. His light found it near the centre of the roof—or at least part of it, impressed in stucco: two concentric circles centred on a cross.

'I'll be damned,' Dutton exclaimed aloud. 'Just like that symbol that the Carnegie expedition found at Uaxactún! Now we know what that was, too.'

Only a portion of the curious symbol was intact, but it was enough for Dutton to see the direction of the arms of the cross.

One pointed straight east. The arm opposite though was slightly bent so that it did not point directly west, but obliquely to one side.

Curious, thought Dutton, following the direction of the bent arm with his eyes and light. His gaze ended at the grand mass of the roof comb. Carefully he walked over to its masonry wall, looked back to make certain he was still in line with the symbol, then turned again to the rough stucco surface. There were painted glyphs under the black mould that coated the stucco! Cautiously Dutton flicked away the dark specks with his fingernails. The only glyph clear enough to read was faint, but Dutton recognized it immediately.

'Incredible,' he muttered aloud. 'The earthquake glyph. My God! The Maya are actually warning me!'

With a start he returned to the job at hand. Venus would be rising soon. No time to waste. Hurriedly Dutton centred the tripod over the place where the centre of the mysterious symbol would have been, then bent to the transit box and unlocked it. Gingerly he slid the heavy instrument out, unscrewed it from the housing, and turned it onto the brass threads atop the tripod. Returning to the box, he took the plumb bob and suspended it from the hook beneath the transit. His light followed its eerie shadow as it slowly swung, then settled over the mark he had made for the centre of the ancient set of circles and cross. With the ease of long experience he levelled and tightened the delicate instrument, clamped the set of degree markers together, brought them into line with the still compass needle, anchored his zero marker there, twisted another knob, and swung the now free telescope towards the east. He was ready for the rising of the morning star.

Dutton's meticulousness in his setting up of the instrument had thrown Rojas and Wilkins into a near frenzy of impatience. Wilkins inched around the end of the roof comb and watched his quarry make a final check of his instrument.

Scraped, bruised, and exhausted by the Herculean task of making the huge rubble pile, the girls had finally reached the level of the beam high in the vault. It proved too rotten to stand on, so they pulled and heaved and wrenched and finally tore it out of the wall. Part of the vault fell with it, half burying Raúl's skeleton and causing Liz to lose her balance. She landed hard on her knees, and when she stood, there was a rip in her jeans and one knee was bloody. But she refused Holly's attempt at help. 'I'm all right. Just push as hard as you can against that red spot.'

Muttering to herself, 'The Golden Age was never the present age,' Holly summoned all the strength she possessed.

With the two girls now firmly anchored on the pile of rubble and both pushing in unison, the heavy capstone moved—only a little at first, but the great slab *had* moved. Excitedly the girls persisted. The stone rocked once, twice, then fell outwards with a loud thump.

'We did it!' Liz cried. The two girls hugged each other.

With Holly close behind, Liz crawled upwards through the

small opening and into the starry night. At the base of the mound they had been in lay the line of a trail, barely visible in the darkness. And there were the girls' bags.

'Wilkins must have wished to make it look as though we wandered here by ourselves,' Holly said. 'It would seem we have no choice but to follow this path if we are going to get help. Fetch the light from your bag.'

Weary, dirty, and fearful again that someone could be watching, the girls stumbled along the irregular trail. Suddenly Liz's flashlight beam picked out a light shape beside the trail ahead.

'A hat!' Holly cried. 'Someone lost a hat.'

'Holly,' Liz sobbed, half hysterical. 'It's Dad's old hat. I'd recognize it anywhere. It *is*! Holly, I just know it is!'

'Look!' Holly answered. 'Up there!' She pointed high above. 'A light on top of the pyramid! Here's a trail going up. Let's go!'

Two hundred feet above the girls Manuel Rojas and Sean Wilkins watched the light that had suddenly appeared on the trail far below. *'Santísima!'* Manuel hissed. 'Who the hell—'

'I don't know,' Wilkins interrupted. 'We can only wait this out and see.'

Both men watched helplessly as the mysterious light bobbed up the pyramid trail closer and closer to their hiding place.

The girls reached the summit, beckoned onwards by Dutton's light. Liz stepped onto the wide roof followed by Holly, who stumbled close behind.

Dizzy with relief, Liz saw her father.

'Dad!' she cried and burst into tears. 'Dad!'

Mel Dutton stood beside his transit dumbfounded. The dim beam showed him his daughter, followed closely by another little girl. Could this be a particularly vivid hallucination? Yet even in the confusion and chaos of the moment, he couldn't help noticing that there was something strangely familiar about the second girl.

When her father didn't answer her, Liz felt a chill shoot up her spine. It was happening just like in her dream: he didn't recognize her! Desperate to break the strange spell, she shouted, 'Dad, we've got to get out of here. Wilkins is going to kill us all!'

The shout seemed to shock Dutton into reality. It was no illusion after all. 'Liz!' he answered her before he could contain himself. He enfolded his daughter in a bear hug, then extended his hand to Holly.

'Dad, this is Holly. She helped get us out of the tomb...there's a skeleton...and when we pushed the red spot...'

'Slower, Liz, you've lost me,' Dutton said. He gave her another hug. 'I was afraid I'd never see you again. How did you get here?'

When Liz started to answer, he interrupted her. 'I want every single detail, but not now. There's something very important that I have to do...this minute. Otherwise I won't have another chance...'

'But, Dad, you don't understand...'

'I do...believe me, I do. Bear with me. In just a few minutes, everything will come together. A moment so rare...'

After a quick check of his wristwatch Dutton took his position behind the instrument, extremely careful not to jar the tripod out of the set level.

In the east the dark sky showed what must have been a billion stars. Easy enough to find the horizon just by *that*,

Dutton thought to himself as he steadied the level telescope to the approximate position he sought. A short wait, then one heavenly body, much brighter than all the rest, winked above the dark and distant tree line, seeming to flash every colour of the rainbow as it lifted into view. Venus, the morning star. The Maya had called it *Xux Ek,* the 'Wasp Star,' or *Chac Ek,* 'Red Star,' and considered it a dread and baleful omen of evil.

Working rapidly, Dutton focused the scope on the quivering light that shone brightly in the dark field of his viewfinder. 'Don't jiggle now!' he cautioned the instrument lovingly. Carefully he adjusted for the slanting path of the bright star and noted the precise angle reading on the engraved silver degree dial.

Meticulously he rechecked his reading and entered the angle averages in his small notebook. Everything checked. He had the alignment. Unfolding the large map he had brought, he laid a protractor on it and drew a thin pencil mark at the proper angle. When he had finished, he looked up. The eastern horizon was beginning to glow. Another day had arrived.

'Dad,' Liz insisted, 'if we stay around here much longer, Wilkins will surely find us. We have to go. Please!'

'It's almost time!' Dutton replied. 'If I leave now, I won't have all my data, and then Wilkins might just as well show up. But I don't want to risk your safety. Both of you go down that path. It will take you to the Jungle Inn. Tell them everything. They'll protect you.'

'We will not leave you here,' Holly said determinedly.

'No,' Liz added. 'Holly's right. We won't leave here without you.'

'Then stay close to me. I'll get us all out of here. I just need to take this transit apart.'

The first sunbeams were hitting the roof comb behind Dutton as he stepped to the transit still focused on the horizon point where Venus had appeared. More out of habit than necessity, Dutton took a last look through the scope.

There on the horizon, so low that it was all but indiscernible along the irregular tree line, lay a more solid shape. Certainly not a tree, Dutton thought with growing excitement. More like a mound, and with a tiny patch of white. Stone all right. That's a mound, he suddenly realized, and quite far—perhaps twenty-five kilometres away.

'That must be it,' he suddenly said aloud, still gazing at the enigmatic bulk in the now bright viewfinder. 'Either that's the Jaguar city itself, or there's a sight line there that will lead beyond to the lost city.' Mel Dutton drew away from the transit and blinked. The sunlight had been too much for his eyes. Everything seemed bluish, and when he turned and raised his eyes towards the girls, he found himself staring down the barrel of Manuel Rojas's rifle. Behind Rojas, covering the girls, stood Sean Wilkins.

'Congratulations, Professor Dutton, on the greatest discovery of your career,' Wilkins offered sarcastically. 'We are fortunate indeed to have witnessed it firsthand.'

By instinct, Dutton took a quick, angry step. Wilkins took one step back and steadied his rifle at the professor. 'Heroism at this time would be most unfitting, my good doctor. You and the young ladies are covered from several positions. Just hand over the notebook and the map.'

'Damn you, Wilkins,' Dutton said, handing Wilkins the notes he had made. 'At least let the girls go. They have no idea what this is all about.'

'I'm really sorry,' replied Wilkins mockingly, 'but, you see, I can't do that now. You understand. Here, I will return your daughter's little trinket. He tossed the jade pendant toward Liz. 'Let's all go down now. Manuel first, then you and the girls.' He beckoned towards Manuel. *'Vámonos, hombre!'*

Shaken and scared, Liz suddenly felt closer to Holly than ever before. Her fingers trembled with emotion as she leaned forward and placed her precious jaguar pendant around Holly's neck. 'Good luck, Holly. Keep this no matter what happens. You're the best friend I've ever had.'

Holly removed her narrow pewter bracelet and slipped it onto Liz's wrist. 'Henceforth,' she whispered, 'there is a bond between us that cannot be broken. I shall never forget you, Liz.'

'What would Poor Richard say at a time like this?' Liz managed with a thin smile.

Holly, with a double take, answered, ' "Help!" probably.'

'Señor Wilkins,' Manuel cried suddenly. 'A helicopter! Look!'

'Very strange,' Wilkins said glancing at the large helicopter scudding across the treetops. We must hurry—immediately.'

He motioned towards the rubble trail as the roar of the chopper reached them.

Dutton whispered quickly to Liz as Manuel began the climb down. 'You and Holly hang back with me. We'll be safest up here. The Maya knew . . .'

Emiliano Guzmán had seen the whole thing from his lookout point atop Temple III. He had done nothing since signaling his companions of Dutton's first approach, and that had been hours ago. Since then everything had seemed under control, even when the girls had unexpectedly come. His viewpoint and the way the voices murmured over the distance had told him all was well. The whole group was beginning to descend. He thought grimly of the fate Wilkins had in store for Dutton and the girls, and wished he could talk Wilkins out of that. As Emiliano began the tortuous descent down the overgrown back of Temple III, he wondered briefly if the helicopter he heard was *federales*. Strange.

Halfway down, Emiliano paused in puzzlement. The bushes were quivering ever so slightly—and there was no wind. He felt movement, but it was below him, seeming to come from the very depths of the earth. Then, suddenly, part of the mound beside the trail rocked, and a whole slope of rubble slid to the level ground below with a crashing and splintering of trees. *Dios mío*, thought Emiliano, *un temblor!* Earthquake. Hurriedly he abandoned his burlap knapsack and water bottle, slipped quickly to safety, and ran towards the woods.

As he reached the edge of the forest, the tall tree immediately beside him wrenched loose. Its rising roots suddenly caught his right leg, pinning him to a protruding boulder of limestone. His face, contorted with panic, pressed into the soft soil.

Frantically Emiliano tried to free his leg or at least turn to see better. No luck. He twisted his head the other way and saw someone approaching cautiously: a woman—a Maya woman.

'Thank God, you are here,' Emiliano cried, grimacing in pain. He turned his head, for Feliciana Uc had said nothing. Struggling to look upward, the last things Emiliano saw were the dark eyes that glittered hate and the piece of tree limb that began to swing downward towards his head.

With Manuel Rojas in the lead the slow procession of five stretched halfway down Temple IV when the first shock hit...a shock high on the Richter scale. The trail below Manuel suddenly vanished with a crash. The man clung desperately to a small tree, but in vain. Frantically his rubber boots sought one—just one—solid piece of the giant pyramid. The tree wrenched free and, with a brief obscenity, Rojas plummeted into the void where the trail had been, as the rest of the group scattered screaming over the undulating slope that remained. There he lay writhing in agony as another layer of debris—tons and tons of hewn stone, tree trunks, and reddish dirt—tore him beyond recognition, then buried him.

'Lie flat!' screamed Dutton at the girls. 'We're much safer here than on the ground! Lie flat!'

Wilkins, wondering why Emiliano—that fool—had set off the dynamite ahead of time, gained the relative safety of level ground alone. Where Dutton or the girls were, he did not know, but at least he had what he had come for, and Dutton

207

The trail below Manuel suddenly vanished with a crash. The
man clung desperately to a small tree, but in vain. Frantically
his rubber boots sought one—just one—solid piece of the giant
pyramid. The tree wrenched free and, with a brief obscenity,
Rojas plummeted into the void where the trail had been.

would never remember those crucial figures in the confusion of the moment. Now only he, Sean Wilkins, could plot the location of the Jaguar city. He patted the bulky packet—the map and Dutton's notebook—in his side pocket and quickly made his way towards camp. He tried to avoid being seen by the helicopter above.

From the helicopter Elaine and Danny had watched the drama unfold below them and were totally mystified.

'What's going on, Mum?' Danny yelled over the noise of the motor as the pilot held the control steady.

'I don't know,' Elaine screamed, 'but there they are, still on the pyramid.'

Danny pointed excitedly. 'Look, they're lying flat! There's Liz, there's her friend Holly, and...and...'

Elaine knew what he was trying to say. 'I just can't believe it!'

'It's Dad! It's really Dad!'

'They're safe! Thank God, they're all safe?' Elaine cried for joy, but the joy returned to fear a moment later. Trees began toppling throughout the jungle. Suddenly part of the pyramid slid away. 'No!'

'It's all right! It's all right, Mum! They're getting up! See? They're all right!'

Elaine pressed her son's hands and burst into tears.

The pilot, his eyes wide with panic, began a slow descent into the manicured grass near the temples, as the horror of what was happening slowly dawned on his two frightened passengers.

From her position on the North Acropolis, Feliciana Uc had

seen it all: the dawn meeting on the summit of the Temple of the Jaguar Priest, Manuel Rojas's fall, Sean Wilkins's cowardly departure. Always with these foreigners there is trouble, she thought. But it was nothing to her. Emiliano Guzmán was dead, bludgeoned to death with her own hands as he lay trapped in the roots of the giant tree. The man she had learned had helped bury Raúl in the tomb. If this man had not helped Wilkins, her husband would still be alive. If only she had learned of the treachery in time to save him. None of her spells, none of her prayers had come to anything. The young people are right, Feliciana sighed, as she headed back to her thatched roof shack. There is no such thing as a helping spirit—no witches, good or bad... From now on I will have nothing to do with such childish games.

Wilkins hardly recognized the ruined camp. A tall *ramón* tree had fallen over one of the tents but, thank the fates, the Suzuki jeep he had rented in Flores was intact and full of petrol. He grabbed a file of incriminating papers from his ruined tent and jumped into the vehicle.

Wilkins had no way of knowing whether the arrival of that military helicopter had anything to do with the Dutton business. With luck, though, even if it was full of *federales,* there was still time to escape. Communication between Tikal and Sayaxché was nonexistent. Certainly the earthquake and the excitement of finding the long-missing archaeologist and the girls would preoccupy the police for a while. He would have a few hours, at least. By that time his Suzuki would be parked inconspicuously among the trucks and Volkswagens on the near bank of the Pasión River, opposite Sayaxché, and he and at least some treasures would be well on their fast journey downstream to the Mexican side of the Usumacinta.

Getting out of Tikal went fairly well. Only two of the hotel people has spotted the Suzuki as Wilkins negotiated it out of the archaeological zone, and they had been left far behind. Now there was only the easy run to Flores and the rougher road to Sayaxché.

On emerging from the helicopter, Danny and Elaine ran towards Liz. Mel and Holly climbed quickly down the last steps of the temple. They all ran towards each other, their hearts pounding, crying and laughing at the same time. As they embraced lovingly, Holly seemed to fit right in. ·

Wilkins's Suzuki pulled into sight of Sayaxché in late afternoon. Nothing unusual here, Wilkins noted, except that everyone was talking about the earthquake. Some said there would be more—and soon.

Wilkins approached two men standing beside a battered old dump truck with its hood open.

'*Amigos,*' Wilkins began genially in Spanish. 'I need two men to help me for about an hour—no more—and I will pay ten *quetzales* to each. Is anyone interested?'

The men looked up, looked at each other, and shrugged, '*Si, ¿por qué no, señor?*—Why not?'

211

'Very well, *hombres,*' Wilkins acknowledged, relieved. 'I want one of you to go over to town and fetch Eduardo Guzmán. I am a friend of his father, Emiliano.'

Wilkins peeled two five-quetzal notes from his roll of money.

'You will find Eduardo's house on the street one block beyond Julio Godoy's hotel, to the right, next to a store that sells hats and rope.'

'I know that store, señor,' interrupted the shorter of the men.

'Very well. Tell Eduardo that Señor Wilkins is at the place where the boat is and that he should bring the motor and a can of petrol for me. And borrow another boat for a few hours. You,' said Wilkins, pointing to the other man, 'come with me.'

Wilkins had never planned to rely solely on the Tikal airstrip as his only means of smuggling antiquities out of Guatemala. Some time ago he had given Emiliano the money to buy a dugout that would hold an outboard motor. It was berthed on the riverbank opposité Sayaxché, just out of sight around the downstream bend. It was there for just such an emergency as this. The escape route into Chiapas was well paved with bribes.

Damn this day, anyway, Wilkins thought. Rojas's death had been the only piece of luck in the whole disastrous morning. Manuel would have had to be eliminated in any case.

He would be at the boat soon. Wilkins and the man left the small roadside store and began the long walk to the boat-mooring downstream. Nearby would be two important stela fragments that he couldn't bear to leave behind, hidden there weeks earlier by Emiliano and Eduardo.

Perhaps it's getting time to move my business elsewhere, Wilkins thought, as he and his companion moved along the riverbank trail. He made his decision then and there. He would move these two pieces out and sell them in the States, then shift his activity to some other part of the world. The Jaguar city could wait a few more years. 'The Mexicans are a civilized people,' Wilkins said aloud to himself. 'So are some Guatemalans—people who know and understand the value of money. But these Maya, even those I have known for a long time, have always kept part of themselves away from me, their

212

faces blank, their thoughts to themselves.' Manuel and the *chicleros* had often thought the Maya were slow, even stupid, Wilkins mused, but he realized now with an uncomfortable feeling that those passive expressions were merely the visible form of an emotion he knew well—contempt. He walked on.

The short man had found Eduardo and was with him at the secret place when Wilkins arrived. Another canoe rocked gently in the water. Eduardo had already secured the heavy Evinrude to the end of Wilkins's hidden dugout. Pleased, Wilkins directed his three helpers to the nearby thicket and started them clearing away the cut foliage that had been carefully placed over the bundles of carved stone.

'Is my father not with you, Señor Wilkins?' Eduardo asked.

'No, *amigo*, he's back at Tikal. He will be here shortly.'

'*Muy bien.*'

The stones are still here, Wilkins thought. Excellent.

Each of the priceless fragments lay securely wrapped in banana-leaf bundles tied by thick rope. Eduardo motioned towards them. 'These are much too heavy, Señor Wilkins. We will need more men to help us move them.'

Wilkins had managed to keep his composure till now. Either Eduardo was trying to delay him or he was simply too stupid to realize the urgency of the matter. . .a matter worth several hundred thousand dollars. Perhaps the helicopter was even on its way here. 'You dumb bastard,' Wilkins shouted in unreasoning rage. '*I'll* help you. We load my boat *now.*'

Eduardo stood quietly and gazed steadily at Wilkins's contorted face. '*Muy bien,*' he said shortly.

It took over an hour to load the cargo, for each stone weighed more than three hundred pounds. They cut wooden poles and used them as levers to pry up the stones and move them along to the dugout. At last all was ready. The boat sat low and with a slight list in the muddy water.

Wilkins, some of his composure restored, bade farewell to Eduardo and the two men, stepped gingerly aboard, and cautiously made his way to the rear of the long boat. He made himself comfortable behind one of the massive bundles.

213

Eduardo stepped into the canoe, grabbed a long oar, and pushed Wilkins. Then the boy raised his eyes in a contemptuous look that escaped Wilkins.

Wilkins waved back at Eduardo and the pair on shore. No use leaving hard feelings. He might return someday and need them again.

Then it happened.

The reeds near where the men stood appeared to be undulating gently, ever so gently at first, then in strong pulsating waves. Suddenly the short man was waving his arms in panic and shouting. Only one word reached Wilkins across the roiling water—*temblor*. Another earthquake.

This one was even stronger than the one that had sent Manuel plunging to his death at Tikal. Wilkins could feel the water sliding out from beneath the boat as if the riverbed were a dish being tilted from side to side by a clumsy giant. Instinctively he jerked the rudder so the boat would remain perpendicular to the large brown waves. For a few seconds he was able to keep the low listing craft under control. Then the bank of silt on the near side of the river split open with a loud thump. At the same time a tall, pearl-grey geyser broke the roiling surface of the river and shot nearly a hundred feet into the air, forcing the boat up in the air and then closer to the shore. In the thundering roar that followed, a huge ceiba tree tilted crazily towards the river, and the handle of the tiller was knocked from Wilkins's hand. Suddenly he felt himself showered with warm water—saltwater. The earthquake must have tapped some long-hidden source.

Even then Wilkins tried not to panic. He told himself he could outswim this. All he had to do was jump free of the twisting boat before it capsized. He lurched towards the bow in order to be as far away from the propeller as possible when he hit the water.

He hesitated for the right moment. It never came.

The huge ceiba caught the boat near the bow, pinning Wilkins's left leg. He felt no pain, only some amazement at the sight of the split end of his white shinbone, pink-streaked with blood, protruding from his wet khaki pants. The boat tilted as

214

if to crash dive to the river bottom. The huge bundles rocked slowly forwards until they came to rest on Wilkins's doomed body.

The grisly cargo vanished into the mud of the river bottom.

Eduardo had survived. His canoe had turned crazily and been upset, throwing the boy into the swirling waters near shore. Vainly he had sought dry ground, then turned and struggled to get onto the capsized boat. With agility born of panic Eduardo catapulted himself onto the splintery hull and sat balanced. Impassively he watched death overtake Wilkins and, despite the danger that remained, he allowed an almost imperceptible smile to play over his stoic features.

Monday, December 25

<big>**I**</big>t was late afternoon of
Christmas Day. Outside the farmhouse in Sturbridge the
sparkling snowflakes drifted in the wind through the cold dark
blue sky. The fire crackled, popped, and spat embers. Melissa
lay stretched out fast asleep in front of the fire screen, her paws
twitching in a dream.

Dinner was over, but the aroma of turkey and gravy, cooked
fruits, cinnamon buns, and assorted pies filled the room. Each
of them proclaimed that this had been the best Christmas
dinner yet, and each had seemed to eat enough for ten.

Mounds of open presents were piled under the glittering
lights of the tree. Nehemiah was playing happily with one of
the ribbons.

Grandpa was reading a magazine. 'Agatha, an article here
says real estate has always been the best investment
historically,' he said without even looking up.

Near the antique hardwood table by the fireplace Liz sat on
the edge of the carpet, reviewing and updating the family
scrapbook with news articles and photographs. There was a

picture in which Mel and Elaine were embracing; one of Elaine, Mel, and Liz beside a gigantic stela; another with the four of them at the New Orleans airport; and even one of Liz and Mel shaking hands with the president of Guatemala. 'I can't believe it!' Liz cried. 'I really can't! She doesn't appear in any of the pictures. She's not here anywhere!'

'How the heck do you explain her then?' said Danny.

Liz pointed at the pewter bracelet on her wrist. 'You saw her, too, didn't you? And so did a lot of other people.' Liz knocked twice hard on the table. 'She was just as real and solid as this maple.'

'Hold it,' Danny said. 'It's time for the news story on us.' He turned on the television set and flipped the dial.

'Christmas is a season for miracles, and that, ladies and gentlemen, is why we have chosen this day to bring you a follow-up on one of the most amazing stories I've covered in my reporting career.' It was Lucy LaBelle again from New Orleans. 'A few weeks ago we brought you the story of Elizabeth Dutton, a thirteen-year-old schoolgirl who ran away from her grandparents' Massachusetts home in a seemingly hopeless attempt to find her archaeologist father. Melville Dutton had been missing since March when he disappeared into the jungles of a remote region of Guatemala. It was a touching but irrational adolescent gesture...

'But Liz Dutton did not fail. Her investigations led her to the reality which had eluded the Guatemalan police: Sean Wilkins, Dutton's former partner, had been selling precious pre-Columbian artifacts on the illegal market and had threatened the life of Professor Dutton who wanted to expose the racket. But Dutton had fled into the jungle where he was very much alive and trying to locate an important new Maya site before it, too, could be looted by his partner's henchmen...'

Lucy LaBelle's TV image faded into a quick shot of the ICAR offices in New Orleans and then to a panning view of Tikal ending with a picture of Mel Dutton and Liz shaking the hand of the president of Guatemala.

'...Thanks to Liz Dutton's courage and luck,' Lucy LaBelle said breathlessly, 'she and her father are now enjoying

217

Christmas at the Dutton family home in Sturbridge, Massachusetts, and Interpol is hot on the trail of a well-organized syndicate of the international art thieves.

'But one mystery still remains. Liz Dutton maintains that she was aided in her adventure by a companion—a little girl who, she says, simply came to life from a portrait at her grandparents' home, announcing herself as one of Liz's ancestors...Holly Hobbie.

'A child's fanciful invention? Maybe. But Professor Dutton says that he saw Holly at Tikal, and several of his colleagues agree that Liz Dutton was accompanied by a youngster answering Holly's description when she visited them shortly after running away from her grandparents' house. Holly existed. Eyewitnesses swear to it. But who was she? The Guatemalan police have found no trace of the girl...

'Perhaps, after all, there are still miracles...This is Lucy LaBelle in New Orleans. Good night and Merry Christmas.'

Danny Dutton switched off the TV in disgust. 'I don't think our friend, Lucy LaBelle, believes in our family miracle.'

'Of course she doesn't, Elaine Dutton intervened. 'Would you in her place?'

Liz sighed. 'Even the Humble Greats know that Holly existed. Freddie sent me her used plane ticket in his letter.'

Liz touched the pewter bracelet that Holly had placed on her arm in exchange for Liz's gift of the jaguar pendant.

'When she left, it was the weirdest moment of my life,' Liz said softly. 'Far scarier than when she first appeared, although I guess it should be the other way around. It's just that I got so used to having her around that I forgot she wasn't going to be here always. She didn't seem to be scared though. I remember...I can still see it. She just said her work was done, and she had to go. I asked her, 'Can we just talk from time to time?' and she said, 'Talk whenever you like. I shall always be listening.' Then she vanished...'

Mel Dutton walked over to his daughter and sat down on the arm of her overstuffed chair. He placed a comforting hand on Liz's shoulder. 'Don't worry, honey. I saw it all too. It doesn't matter if no one here really believes us. To the Maya way of thinking, Holly's role makes perfect sense. Maya sorcerers often call on a man's ancestors to help him battle against the spirits of the night. Perhaps that's what you did in a way. You wanted help so much that you must have pulled "Old Aunt Holly" right out of her picture frame.'

Elaine Dutton came over to the two of them. Her husband pulled her down onto his lap and both of them fell to the floor in the process, laughed, and then embraced.

'Puh-*leeze,*' Danny protested with mock dismay, 'no lechery in front of the children. It ruins their appetites.'

Liz rolled her eyes skyward in an exaggerated imitation of Holly's expression when she had a proverb to deliver. 'A clean mind in a healthy body...can always eat.'

I'll say one thing,' Danny retorted. 'Holly Patches certainly added to your repertoire of expressions. I don't know what you'll do without her.'

'I don't either, but at least we have some friends in common,' Liz replied, feeling inside her pocket for the tickets to the New Year's rock concert that Herman and Freddie had sent her for Christmas.

Melville smiled. 'As *your* friend, Poor Richard, said, 'The noblest question in the world is, What Good may I do in it?' Incidentally, we have a surprise for you...We're going back to Guatemala.'

Elaine added, 'Dad and Herschel Goodman are going to be leaving in mid-January to locate the Jaguar city. Dad is sure he can find it now, and we're all going with them. That's if Liz hasn't had her fill of the Maya already...'

'Of course not,' Liz answered eagerly.

'I think it won't hurt you and Danny to miss a term at school, and Hal Abbot can handle the business for a few months. I'm going to be writing a book about Maya mythology. Won't it be exciting to live in a country where the people's everyday lives are still permeated by faith in the supernatural?'

Liz raised her eyebrows in astonishment, and then she, Danny, and her father broke into laughter.

' "Where folks believe in witches, witches are," ' Liz said as soon as she could get her breath. 'Now I know what Holly meant when she had me give you that message. It's a special kind of believing...

'Dad,' Liz whispered, her face suddenly dark and solemn. 'Could we go up and see Holly?'

Mel took his daughter's hand, and they started up the stairs, Nehemiah leading the way.

Mel lit a candle and held it up to the wall where Holly's picture was hung. Moving closer, Liz flushed with colour. 'Dad! Dad, look!' Mel came closer and squinted to see the painting in greater detail. There, around Holly's neck, was the jade pendant with its precisely carved jaguar face.

Mel put his arm around his daughter. The moment was too big for words. They felt as if some great change had occurred in their lives. As they rejoined the happy celebration, Liz couldn't resist stroking Holly's bracelet. She felt that Holly was near and could hear again the words with which they had exchanged gifts. 'There is a bond between us...'

*T*he small figure, peering through the bay window into the old house, had been watching the Dutton family enjoy their most memorable Christmas. Nehemiah sensed the presence, his ears alert and tail flicking slowly. He leaped onto the window seat, staring out at someone he recognized. Holly, satisfied that all was right, picked up her colourful bag and set out across the new snow toward the bus.

The Greyhound bus was parked at its roadside shelter in Old Sturbridge Village, facing down the clean white winding country road lined by bare trees. The driver listened to the engine, checked his windshield, tilted his cap, and closed the door, not noticing that behind the bus a little girl was approaching.

Holly was moving as fast as she could, yet as gracefully as if she were moving in smooth slow motion. The heavy carpetbag in her arms almost seemed to pull her along. Her red hair trailed out from under her bonnet, streaming in the wind. Reaching the bus just as it was pulling away, she shrugged her shoulders once and with a misty smile dissolved through the solid bus.

Settling down by a window, Holly straightened her bonnet and caught her breath. She lifted the jade pendant Liz had given her and admired it with a slight, forlorn glance. She would never forget it—or her friend. Looking out of the bus window, she laughed gently and blew a soft kiss in the direction of the Dutton farmhouse.

Nothing that was worthy in the past departs;
no truth or goodness realized by man
ever dies, or can die.

Thomas Carlyle